"Keep do

After making sure Danny was okay, Harper ducked her head.

When the truck rammed them, Luca did his best to hold the Jeep steady, but the impact and the icy road sent them swerving. He righted the vehicle before it slid into the ditch flanking the road. If he allowed that to happen, he doubted he'd be able to get it out, and there was no question that the men were heavily armed.

He saw Harper brace herself for a second hit.

"What are we going to do?" Her voice was calm, but he knew she understood the consequences if the men chasing them caught up with them.

Men like that would show no mercy, not even to a wounded woman and a young boy. They'd already proven just how far they were willing to go to retrieve the drugs.

"We're going to outrun them," he said. "If we can't do that, we'll think of something else."

Just what that something else was, he had no idea.

Jane M. Choate dreamed of writing from the time she was a small child when she entertained friends with outlandish stories complete with happily-ever-after endings. Writing for Love Inspired Suspense is a dream come true. Jane is the proud mother of five children, grandmother to ten grandchildren and staff to one cat who believes she is of royal descent.

Books by Jane M. Choate

Love Inspired Suspense

Keeping Watch
The Littlest Witness
Shattered Secrets
High-Risk Investigation
Inherited Threat
Stolen Child
Secrets from the Past
Lethal Corruption
Rocky Mountain Vendetta
Christmas Witness Survival
Rocky Mountain Survival
Rocky Mountain Kidnapping

Visit the Author Profile page at LoveInspired.com.

ROCKY MOUNTAIN KIDNAPPING

JANE M. CHOATE

LOVE INSPIRED SUSPENSE

INSPIRATIONAL ROMANCE

LOVE INSPIRED® SUSPENSE
INSPIRATIONAL ROMANCE

Recycling programs for this product may not exist in your area.

ISBN-13: 978-1-335-95724-5

Rocky Mountain Kidnapping

Love Inspired
22 Adelaide St. West, 41st Floor
Toronto, Ontario M5H 4E3, Canada
www.LoveInspired.com

Printed in Lithuania

MIX
Paper | Supporting responsible forestry
FSC® C021394

If God be for us, who can be against us?
—*Romans* 8:31

To my grandchildren:
Hannah, Reynna, Christopher, Brigham, Isaac,
Amelia, Hudson, Julie, Wyatt, Charlotte.

ONE

Muffled plinks of icy rain pelleted her head and shoulders. So tired and cold was she that she scarcely noticed. She dismounted and led the big gelding to the barn. "You came through for me today, boy," she told Hank with an affectionate pat to his sleek neck. "Just like you always do."

Having just returned from a grueling search-and-rescue mission, Harper Sloan was ready for a hot shower and a hot meal. The mission, finding a lost Boy Scout in the Rocky Mountains, had been successful, but not without cost. One of the volunteers had been badly hurt in a fall. She'd received word that he was being treated in the hospital where he'd been airlifted. The boy, scared but unhurt, had been reunited with his much-relieved parents.

Dusk was just falling, making it more than twelve hours since she'd departed from home early that morning.

Home.

She never thought she would ever again refer to the twenty-thousand-acre Colorado ranch as home since she had left it nearly six years ago. Now it belonged to her son, Danny.

Who would have thought that her father, shortly before his death six months ago, would leave it to her son? Her father, the Judge, had kicked her out of the only home she'd ever known when she refused to give up the baby she'd borne.

They'd parted on harsh words, with a vow on her part never to return. Only when he'd summoned her to his death-bed had she come back. Learning that he had made arrange-ments to leave the ranch to Danny had softened her heart, though only partially. The real cause of their estrangement, when he'd forced her to annul her very brief marriage, was a barrier that would forever remain between them.

She shook off the unwanted memories and went about seeing to Hank. In the shelter of the barn, with its famil-iar scents of oiled leather, horseflesh, and straw and away from the stinging barbs of snow and ice, she removed the heavy saddle and began rubbing him down. His neigh of pleasure soothed away the rough edges of what had been an extremely long day. She stroked Hank's soft nose and was rewarded with a nuzzle to her neck.

A stirring in the air behind her alerted her that she was not alone. Just as she registered it, a hand clamped over her mouth. She breathed through her nose, but fear and panic made it difficult to fill her oxygen-starved lungs.

"If you want to see your son again, keep quiet and lis-ten," a voice said as she struggled to free herself.

At the mention of Danny, she went still.

"That's better." The man removed his hand from her mouth, only to settle both hands on her shoulders in a bruis-ing grip.

Harper knew when to fight and when to bide her time. This was a time for the latter. She pulled in a long breath and asked, "What have you done with my son?"

Her captor leaned in closer. Even the redolent smells of horses and sweet hay couldn't mask his foul breath. It smelled of stale smoke and decay. It was all she could do not to gag from it.

"We have your son and your housekeeper. If you want them to live, you'll do as I say."

Her decision to bide her time was forgotten at the idea of her son in this man's hands. She drew back her booted foot to hit him in the ankle. Unfortunately, she lacked the leverage to do much damage.

"What did you do to him?" Harsh breaths clawed their way out of her throat. She wrenched free and turned to face him. And gasped. His face was covered with a latex mask, its grotesque features leering at her.

His hold on her broken, he muttered something crude then, quick as a snake ready to bite, pulled a knife from a scabbard at his waist and held it against her neck, nicking her throat. "He's fine. As long as you do what I say, he'll stay that way."

It cost her to assume a meek pose, but she forced her body to relax. "Please. Tell me what you want."

"We want you to retrieve a package."

That was the second time he'd used the word *we*. Was there a second man nearby? And what did he mean by a *package*? Drugs? It was no secret that drugs were invading the area at an alarming pace.

He lowered the knife, giving her a small bit of latitude to attack. It was now or never, and she pulled free from his grasp. When he raised an arm to cuff her, she used her forearm to block the move and grabbed his arm with her other hand, cranking his elbow up past the breaking point. His shoulder separated clearly, a popping sound telling her it was broken.

He fell to the ground, clutching his shoulder and yelling invectives at her.

Before she could jump on top of him and demand answers, she was lifted off her feet and thrown to the corner of the stall. She landed hard on her side. So, there was a second man after all.

The second masked assailant yanked her up by her hair. "You're good," he said, "but not good enough to take on the two of us. Now listen and listen good." He pulled her hair so that pain screamed through her scalp. "There's a package in the mountains. We have the coordinates. All you have to do is retrieve it and bring it to us. Then you'll get your son back."

She knew better than to believe him, but she would play along. "Why don't you get it by yourselves?"

"The wind could have sent it anywhere. You have the reputation of finding people. That means you can find this package and bring it to us."

By now, the first man had gotten to his feet and advanced on her. "You broke my shoulder."

He fisted his hand and reared back his good arm, ready to strike, when his partner stopped him. "We need her. She won't be any use to us if you make her your punching bag."

"Someday," the first aggressor said, "you and me are gonna meet up again. When we do, you'll be sorry you messed with me." He pulled a crumpled sheet of paper from his pocket. "Here're the coordinates of where the package should be."

She had the urge to laugh hysterically. The record-breaking storm with heavy snow and high winds that had blown in earlier and still raged could have sent the package anywhere. "You're asking the impossible."

"You'd better hope not. We've got your boy and the old lady. Their lives depend on you getting us what we want. And if you want them back, you'd better not call the cops."

She had been cold before, but it in no way matched the icy sensation that spread to every part of her body now.

Danny. In the hands of men like these. A lump lodged in her throat, constricting her breathing. Prayers crowded her mind along with a fear so intense that she was in danger of shutting down.

But she couldn't give in to that luxury.

Danny needed her.

"How am I supposed to find a package in the middle of a snowstorm?"

"You're some kind of hotshot search-and-rescue expert, aren't you? With your boy as the prize, I don't think you'll have any problem finding what we're looking for."

With that, he and his partner exited the barn.

To Harper's shame, she realized she'd scarcely given Vera, her housekeeper and her foreman's wife, a thought. Vera was pushing sixty-five and had arthritis. She couldn't handle the rough treatment Harper feared she'd face at the hands of these men. At the same time, Harper was grateful to have someone there who would look after Danny.

The enormity of what had happened hit her in a second wave of terror. Danny had been taken. Her son. Her reason for living. A buzzing noise filled her head. As a cry ripped from her throat, a cold sweat gathered at the base of her neck.

Enough.

This was no time to give in to hysterics. A grunt came from the far corner of the barn. After arming herself with a pitchfork, she followed the sound.

Her foreman, Chuck Dawson, lay there, mouth gagged and hands and feet bound. A gash on his forehead wept blood.

She untied his hands and feet and removed the gag from

his mouth, then pulled a kerchief from her coat pocket and wrapped it around the wound on his forehead. "What happened?"

He cleared his throat. "I'm sorry as I can be, Harper. There were four of them. The two that just left and two others. They took Danny and my Vera."

She'd been told that by the abductors, but this time the words came to her as though from a great distance, and she struggled to form a response. What *could* she say to the news that her son had been kidnapped? There were no words for it.

The mind's self-defense mechanism took hold, turning hysterical fear into shock. It was that, the shock and the coldness that it brought with it, that allowed her to get beyond those first terrible moments. She wanted to hold on to it, to use it as others would a drug.

Never, though, had she experienced this mind-numbing fear of hearing that Danny had been taken. She dry heaved, waves of icy cold then fiery heat coursing through her relentlessly. Surely she hadn't heard correctly. The cold had corrupted her hearing. That was it. No one had taken Danny. She held on to the thought, even while knowing it was false.

She wasn't certain how they got out of the barn. She didn't remember walking to the house. On some level, she noted that Chuck had draped a heavy arm over her shoulder, whether as support for himself or for her, she didn't know. The blizzard buffeted them, but she scarcely noticed.

Operating on automatic, she put one foot in front of the other. Every hair at the nape of her neck pulled tight. At the same time, her muscles readied for a battle for which she didn't yet know the rules. But there would be a battle. She knew that. Even as she knew it was one she could not fight alone.

They entered through the back door that led to the mud-room and then the kitchen. The front door was rarely used. Inside the mudroom, she shed her hat, coat, scarf and gloves before sitting on a stool and pulling off her boots. A rubber tray sat on the floor to hold wet boots and shoes.

First things first. She had to see to the gash on Chuck's head. She retrieved the first aid kit from a cupboard and set about washing and tending the wound then applying a square of gauze.

"That should do it," she said.

Chuck following her, she walked through the kitchen to the library, her favorite room in the house. A fire blazed in the ceiling-high fireplace that occupied a good portion of one wall. Floor-to-ceiling shelves on the other three walls held a collection of her father's books that ranged from the classics to true crime to satire. When she and Danny had moved in, she'd stocked the lower shelves with books he would enjoy. Normally, she found the room's warmth welcoming, but there was no welcome in it today. Not for her.

She sat in the massive chair behind the equally massive desk, the one her father had occupied for so many years and one she usually avoided. Today, it seemed the right choice. She didn't trust herself to speak. Not yet. Another minute, maybe two, and she'd be able to put two words together without giving way to despair.

Deliberately, she called up memories of happier times. The mental pictures sustained her.

Danny riding his first pony.

Danny playing in a snow drift.

Danny staring up at her in bewilderment and joy upon feeling the first snow on his face.

So lost was she in images from the past that she failed to hear Chuck's insistent voice.

"Harper, you've got to snap out of it," her foreman said. "Danny and Vera need you."

The mention of her son penetrated the fog under which she'd been operating. "Take me through it," she said. "Slowly."

Chuck put a hand to his head and rubbed his temples as though to ease a headache. She had an impulse to do the same but resisted. She couldn't give in to weakness.

He squatted in front of her. "It was like this, you see." She normally found Chuck's drawl soothing, but now it grated on her.

"Four men walked right into the barn, bold as you please. Two took off to the house while the other two hogtied me slicker than a calf at a rodeo. When I tried to fight, one slugged me with the butt of his pistol, and I got this for my trouble." Gingerly, he touched his forehead. "The two that headed for the house came back with Danny and Vera."

She listened, her terror growing with every word. Her mouth went dry; conversely, her hands were wet with sweat.

"The two who took Danny and Vera. What did they look like?"

"One was a big dude. At least six-three, maybe more. The other was smaller, though not by much. I didn't get a look at their faces since they were wearing masks. You saw."

She gave a terse nod. "What else?"

"They were carrying some heavy-duty firepower. One was toting a Remington 7 mm Magnum. The other had a 1911 Colt .45."

Admiration for the weapons rang in Chuck's voice.

"Once you're finished gushing over the guns," she snapped, "maybe we can get back to the subject of Danny and Vera being kidnapped."

Her foreman flushed. "Sorry. Didn't mean to go on like that."

"No. I'm the one who's sorry. I shouldn't have come down on you that way." Chuck was a gunsmith as well as the foreman of the ranch. Of course, he'd noticed the men's weapons. "And it helps knowing what they were carrying. Tells us something about the men." She needed more. "Was there any other clue as to who they were?"

"Not a one. If I knew, don't you think I'd tell you? They have Vera." His voice broke, along with her heart.

Her breathing went shallow. Her heart ached for both Vera and Danny. Five-year-old Danny. Her son. The light of her life. Taken by thugs, probably drug dealers.

"When?" she demanded.

"Just before you found me. They showed up like a black cloud blocking out the sun."

It was a mistake. Any moment, he'd burst through the kitchen door, grinning with the smile that showed a wobbly tooth and calling, "Mommy. Where are you?"

The scenario was so vivid that she looked around to make sure she hadn't dreamed the conversation between her and Chuck, a horrible dream from which she would wake and then scold herself for allowing her runaway imagination to get the best of her.

But the worry on Chuck's face told her that it was no dream. "Harper, honey, I know it's a lot to take in, but you have to try. Danny and Vera need us." Chuck laid a hand on her arm. "Coming apart at the seams won't help them. Or us."

Once again, Harper resisted the urge to rub her temple, refusing to acknowledge the headache that was brewing. Headaches were her enemy, especially if they grew into migraines. She couldn't allow that to happen. There were no tears now, only an icy fear that had spread through her entire body.

Fear was no stranger to her. In her search-and-rescue efforts, she'd experienced it plenty of times. Never, though, had she experienced the chilling fear of learning that her own son had been taken. With dark brown hair, a smattering of freckles and a smile that was as irrepressible as his cowlick, he was impossible not to love. Especially when you added in a tender heart and a sweet nature.

The fear wouldn't disappear, but she could and would use it. Fierce determination made her voice brisk. "Take me through it again."

Chuck repeated the story, nearly verbatim. "They said it would go worse for Danny if you called the police," he added.

Silently, she uttered a prayer, the words running together incoherently, but she knew the Lord heard them and knew of her need. *Please, Lord. Watch over Danny. He's just a little boy.* With a prayer said, she felt mind and body begin to work together to decide upon a course of action.

"If I had to guess," Chuck said, "I'd say that these guys are not only first-rate with most weapons but also enjoy what they do." There was no one better at sizing up people than Chuck, and she trusted his instincts.

What she was learning was frightening her more and more. The silent prayer she'd offered earlier had soothed the ragged edges of her heart, but it hadn't banished the fear. Nothing could do that but having her son back in her arms.

She opened her laptop and entered the coordinates the kidnapper had given her. Smack dab in the center of the storm system that was intensifying. After checking for wind speed and direction, she did a series of calculations to determine where the package would most likely be now.

That was the easy part. Now for the hard part.

"We can't do this on our own," she said. They needed help. Professional help.

"You going to go to the police? Despite what the men said?" She heard the tension in Chuck's voice. They were both strung so tight she could almost hear the snap of nerves.

"No." She had someone else in mind. A man who would eat kidnappers for breakfast. If he'd help her. The last time she'd seen him, they'd parted with angry words, his, and tears, hers.

Even now, nearly six years later, grief squeezed her heart at how it had gone down. With an impatient jerk of her head, she pushed it aside. This was not the time for regrets. Not when Danny was missing.

"I have to go out," she said.

Chuck blinked at her abrupt tone. "Now?"

"Now. Hold down the fort. I'll be back by night."

"Don't you think we ought to talk about what we're going to do?"

"There'll be time enough for talking later." When they got Danny back. She didn't allow herself to use the word *if*.

A mother's guilt sluiced through her as she prepared for the hour-long trip. She hadn't been at home, caring for Danny. No, she was out playing hero, rescuing another child. If she'd been at home, could she have stopped the kidnapping? She didn't know. She'd never know.

The only thing she knew for certain was that she'd have fought like a mama grizzly to protect him.

It was only by accident that she knew of Luca Brady's whereabouts. An online article related the story of the Denver division of S&J Security/Protection opening a satellite office in a neighboring town. Luca Brady had been listed as one of ten operatives.

If she needed to beg, she would.

Luca Brady didn't like babysitting assignments. It didn't matter that his boss had personally asked him to take the case. It didn't matter that he was protecting a beauty pageant contestant. It still amounted to babysitting.

One more hour and he'd be off the clock. The pageant would be over. His protectee would likely move on to the next pageant and the one after that. Frankly, he couldn't see the importance of something that seemed no more than a popularity contest, but the girl's parents had paid S&J big bucks to protect their daughter.

He had a week of leave, and he intended to use it by going backpacking, away from everything and everyone. He'd take his cell, but otherwise he intended to cut himself off from the demands of civilization. After checking in with Gideon Stratham, the supervisor of S&J's western division, he headed home and began packing.

An hour later, he was checking his gear a final time when a knock at the door had him gritting his teeth. He didn't care who it was; he was off the clock and intended to stay that way.

He opened the door and felt his heart leaping in his chest before coming to an abrupt stop as he stared at the woman who had once been his wife. Her father, a judge and the most powerful man in the area, had forced Harper to get their short marriage annulled. Either that or, he threatened, he would see to it that Luca spent the next five years in prison. The Judge had always ruled her with an iron fist, one unhampered by love.

Luca's crime? When Luca had seen the Judge using a

whip on a horse, he'd taken the whip away from him and slashed him in the face with it. The Judge threatened him with an assault charge. Luca had argued with Harper, telling her he'd take his chances in court, but she'd refused to listen. They'd parted on angry words, with her telling him that she didn't take orders from him. That had been a recurring problem throughout their relationship.

Over the years, Luca regretted acting as he had. He was no better than her father.

Luca forced the memories away and stared at Harper. She was more beautiful than ever. That was his first thought. His second was that she looked brittle enough to break, with lines of strain etched on her face. Still, it didn't detract from her beauty. Her cheeks had lost the roundness of youth, and her features were delicately formed. With blond hair framing her face in loose curls and brown eyes, she was truly lovely.

"Harper."

"Luca."

It seemed that neither of them was able to get out more than the other's name.

Finally, he managed, "What are you doing here?" He flushed at his less than gracious tone and gestured her inside to a chair.

She refused the offer of a seat. "I need your help."

An odd request, he thought, seeing as how he hadn't seen her in almost six years. "What is it?"

"My son..." Her voice choked, and she stopped, obviously unable to go on.

He did his best not to react to the news that she had a son even as a spate of jealousy surged through him. She'd obviously moved on since the annulment and had remarried.

"My son's been kidnapped."

He froze. Memories assailed him of a kidnapping in Afghanistan, where he'd been deployed with the rangers. The local police chief's daughter had been taken by a band of terrorists. If he refused to work with them, she would be killed in the most horrible way possible.

Luca and his unit had brought the girl home, but they'd lost two good men in doing so.

"Will you help me?" she asked, drawing him back to the present. She caught her tongue between her teeth, a tell he recalled from years ago. It told him that it had cost her dearly to ask for help.

He didn't bother answering. They both knew he would. "Tell me what you know."

She told him what little she knew. How she'd come back from a search-and-rescue mission to find two men waiting for her in the barn. "One clamped a hand over my mouth and said they had taken Danny." She swallowed. "My son."

"Any description?"

"They were wearing masks. The first one put a piece of paper in my hands, telling me it held the coordinates of where a package was." She drew a breath. "I wanted to go after them first thing, but I knew I needed help."

He could only imagine. If it was his child, he'd be champing at the bit to find him and then dispatch the people who had taken him.

"Are you still at the ranch?" The ranch had belonged to her father, a hard man who had kept Harper under his thumb and out of his heart.

She nodded.

"Give me a couple of minutes to grab a few things." Though he'd already packed, he wanted to add some special gear. Five minutes later, he returned with another pack, this one filled with flash bangs, zip ties, and though he was carrying his usual Glock, he added a Sig Sauer P320. Both were semiautomatic service pistols. He favored the Glock as it was what he'd used as a ranger, but the Sig was equally as deadly.

"Let's go." He hefted both packs over his shoulders.

He resisted the urge to draw her to him. He resisted the urge to promise that everything would be all right. He resisted the urge to ask why she'd come to him after nearly six years. He had no right to do any of those things.

He'd worked long and hard, but never successfully, to forget her. How could he forget the girl—now woman— who had occupied his heart ever since he was a callow youth? Sure, he'd gone out with other women since their marriage ended, but things rarely went beyond the first date.

None of that mattered, and so he focused on what he could do. Find her son.

He knew her father, the Judge, had died last year. If he'd been alive, it would have twisted his gut to know that Harper had gone to him, Luca, for help. Impatiently, he brushed that away. Now wasn't the time for petty thoughts.

Along with emotions he had no right feeling, questions tumbled around in his mind, like what her husband thought of her coming to Luca for help. Was he on board with that? What would he think when Luca showed up?

He forced everything from his mind except the only thing that mattered. Helping the woman he'd once loved. The woman who, for a very short while, had been his wife. There'd be time enough for questions later. For now, he and Harper needed to get back to the ranch.

Wanting to have his own vehicle, he persuaded her to ride with him, telling her that he'd have someone bring her truck to the ranch.

"How did you find me?" he asked her when they'd settled into his vehicle.

"Are you kidding? S&J is big news. I saw your name in the paper when the company brought down the lieutenant governor."

A photojournalist had found herself a target when she'd unknowingly taken a picture of Colorado's lieutenant governor with a mobster. When she'd turned to S&J for help, they had proven the LG was corrupt.

Taking him down had called national attention to the company. And though Luca hadn't been in on the actual takedown, he'd been involved in the case, and his name had been brought up, along with his military service.

The last thing he'd wanted was publicity. He'd had enough of it to last a lifetime during his years in the rangers. During one deployment, he'd been heralded a hero for saving six of his men from a mortar attack. He'd done his best to keep a low profile. Medals didn't make a hero. Not in his book. Standing by his men came first.

It was with relief when he'd accepted the job at S&J. Its founders, brother and sister Jake Rabb and Shelley Rabb Judd, had decided to open a satellite office in Colorado.

It was a nod to his abilities, one he was determined to live up to. The job gave him the opportunity to use his skills to help those who couldn't help themselves, just as he'd done in the rangers.

The drive to the ranch took less than an hour, but it felt interminable. He and Harper, once so close, had nothing to say to each other. Every subject that came to mind felt loaded with past pain and recrimination.

"Tell me about Danny," he said when the silence grew unbearable.

"Asking a mother to tell you about her son is dangerous. I could talk about him for hours. Days."

"Does he look like you?" Luca asked, interrupting the flow of her thoughts.

"No. He takes after his father."

"How old is he?"

She didn't answer right away.

"Harper?"

When she answered, it was with defiance. "Five. He just turned five."

Luca went still. "Five? Does that mean—?"

"Yes, Luca. Danny's your son."

His son?

The revelation that he had a son filled him with an inexplicable joy. At the same time, outrage threatened to overtake him. How dare Harper have kept that from him!

By the time they arrived at the ranch, he was still grappling with the news that this mission was to rescue his own son. *His son.* The words had both the power to thrill him and to fill him with fear. His son's life depended upon him.

Never had an op been more important.

TWO

Luca ignored the ever-growing strain between him and Harper as they readied for the journey before dawn the following morning. Though he had been anxious to get started last night, he recognized the wisdom in waiting until morning.

Grateful that she didn't try to engage in small talk, he asked questions in a clipped voice; she responded in an equally clipped one.

The thickening tension did not bode well for what lay ahead. He and Harper had to work together if they were to save their son. Questions hovered on his tongue, but he couldn't get past the biggest one of all.

Why?

Why hadn't she told him he had a son?

He feared giving voice to it. If he did, he might not be able to halt the anger that was even now streaming through him.

He watched as she packed their gear in canvas knapsacks. Having ridden in the mountains her whole life, she knew what to bring, what to leave. He understood that preparation could make the difference between living and dying, just as it had while he was deployed.

There'd been a heated discussion last night between

Chuck, the ranch foreman, and Harper. When Chuck said that he needed to help rescue Vera and Danny, Harper had gently vetoed it, reminding him that he had a head wound and wasn't up to what was sure to be a hard ride in the mountains. After the initial argument, Chuck had given in.

Though the foreman was in good shape for being in his sixties, Luca agreed with her decision. Also, he'd detected a certain coldness directed his way from Chuck. It was better all around if he stayed behind.

In the barn, Luca adjusted his eyes to the dim light.

"I picked out Claude for you," Harper said. "He's a good steady mount."

Luca eyed the gelding who must have stood a good seventeen hands. A big animal with long withers and a strong chest. He patted the horse's neck. "We're going to get along fine."

Claude gave a sharp whinny as though in agreement.

"He's one of my favorites," Harper said. "He's not a show-off like that little filly over there," she said, pointing to a stall where a high-stepping filly pranced about. "But he's sure-footed and reliable, and he'll get you where you want to go."

"Can't ask for more than that," Luca said and patted the gelding's neck, noting the strength beneath the glossy mane. "Let's get it done."

In the rangers, getting the job done was everything. It didn't matter if you were injured. It didn't matter if the temperature was sixty degrees below zero or 125 degrees in the shade. Nothing mattered but the mission. You got the job done. Period. No excuses. No apologies. Failure not an option.

Rangers lead the way. The ranger motto hadn't changed in decades.

Depending on anyone was anathema to him, but he recognized that Harper was in charge here. She knew the territory, knew the weather patterns, knew the trails. Part of being a good soldier was recognizing superior skills in a comrade. The Colorado Rockies were breathtaking, but they were also treacherous with sharp canyons and sheer cliffs. Add to that a windchill factor well below freezing, and you had a formula for disaster for the unprepared and unwary.

For now, he and Harper were partners. They had to depend on each other. Without that, they stood little chance of getting Danny back safely. Thoughts of his son caused his jaw to harden.

Once Danny was safe, he and Harper would have a talk, one long overdue to his way of thinking, and come to some agreement about custody. Until then, he would focus on bringing his boy home and then settling the score with whoever had taken him. Though he didn't believe in vengeance, he did believe in justice.

Using the coordinates that the attackers had given Harper, they headed west. There was little chance the package would be in the designated location, but they had to start somewhere. There had been a break in the storm, and for a while the towering pines allowed rays of stingy sunshine to seep through. As the day wore on, what little sunlight there was waned even more. The sky grew ever darker as clouds bloated with snow moved in. It didn't take a meteorologist to predict that the storm system was gathering strength.

He tipped his hat down low to protect his face from the constant wind.

Though he was grateful for the relatively easy ride, he knew it wouldn't last. The grade was steepening, a gradual rise that could take a person by surprise if he wasn't paying attention.

"You doing okay?" she called over her shoulder.

"Yeah."

He knew Harper was bothered by his monosyllabic answers, but he didn't have it in him to give more. He wasn't ready to talk. Not about Danny. Not about anything.

Claude was an old hand in the knee-deep snow. He moved with a steady gait that told Luca he was accustomed to the weather. Luca huddled deeper in his coat against the stiffening wind.

The going grew rougher the higher they climbed. Boulders littered the trail. When it became apparent that the horses couldn't go any farther, not without risk of injury, Harper called a halt and dismounted. After unloading the saddlebags and making sure the animals were well fed, she sent them home with a slap to their flanks.

"I'm guessing they know their way back to the ranch," he said.

She gave a short nod.

Luca surveyed the supplies she'd pulled from the saddlebags. Without the horses, he and Harper would have to carry their gear themselves.

She divided the supplies into equal amounts and started loading their knapsacks. When Luca stopped her, she looked up in surprise.

"Give me some of that," he said after she'd filled his knapsack and started on her own. "I still have room in mine."

"It's not a question of room," she said. "It's a question of weight."

"That's right. I weigh considerably more than you and can carry more."

"I can manage." The stiffness in her voice said that she wasn't about to take any favors from him.

"I know. But this will be more efficient."

"All right," she said in a grudging tone. "Thanks. I owe you one."

"You don't owe me a thing. This is for Danny."

Working together, they redistributed the supplies. He caught her wincing as she hefted the pack on her shoulders. Even with him taking the lion's share of the items, he knew the pack was heavier than was comfortable for her, but she didn't complain.

Luca watched as her face creased, watched how she bit the inside of her cheek. She didn't have to give voice to her agony over Danny's abduction. He shared it. He wanted to ease her mind, but there was nothing he could say that wouldn't sound foolish. Drug runners had their son. It was as simple as that.

He would make them pay. That was also simple.

"Of course, the drugs won't be at the site, but we have to start somewhere. If my calculations are correct, they would have been carried five or more miles to the north. The only way to know for sure is to explore. That's the tricky part. If I'm wrong, it'll waste time." She didn't have to say that time was a luxury they didn't have. The more time that slipped by while the kidnappers had Danny, the less likely that they would get him back safely.

The trail steepened, the air growing thinner. He worked to take long, slow breaths. The bitter cold, though, didn't cooperate as it propelled what felt like shards of glass down his throat with every inhale. The exhale was scarcely better.

Harper slowed the pace, and though he wanted to speed things up, he recognized the wisdom of the move.

When they reached a narrow ledge that ran across a mountain ridge, she stopped. "Things can get pretty hairy through here. You up for it?"

Was she remembering the time years ago when they'd

fallen into a narrow canyon and had had to climb their way out? They'd had to scale a cliff, the height of which had sent him into a near panic. He was glad to say he'd over-come his fear of heights. Mostly.

Luca appreciated her concern, but he had not forgiven her for keeping his son from him. They'd deal with that later. When Danny was safe. Until then, better that he kept his feelings to himself. If they spilled out, he feared anger would take the place of the cooperation they needed to bring Danny home.

"I'm game."

He'd navigated his share of cliffs and ledges while de-ployed and then again as an S&J operative, but he had never grown to like the sheer drops that accompanied them. Give him a HALO jump to make, and he was your man. The high-altitude, low-opening jumps from a plane thousands of feet in the air didn't bother him. *Pretend you're on a jump*, he told himself.

Harper must have sensed his tension for she turned slightly. "Relax."

He gave a curt nod. Was his unease so obvious? Perhaps she'd heard it in the quickening of his breathing.

"Don't look down."

Of course, he looked.

Big mistake. The drop was hundreds of feet. *You're a ranger*, he reminded himself. *An army ranger. You've faced down tangos a lot more dangerous than one measly ledge, even if it is two hundred feet above the ground.*

He kept his gaze focused on the straight line of Harper's back as she strode fearlessly across the narrow strip.

Luca felt the ground shift. One moment, it was firm beneath his feet; in a heartbeat, it caved in, sending him toward the ledge. He slipped in a patch of slick mud and tumbled over, barely managing to catch the stump of a scrub oak on his way down.

Harper scrambled to the spot where he'd fallen and stretched out her arm. "Give me your hand."

He resisted. She couldn't possibly pull him up. He was too heavy for her. He knew it; if she was smart, she knew it, too.

"Do it," she snapped.

Despite his misgivings, he caught her hand.

"We can do this," she said. "All you have to do is to hold on."

He felt the strain in her arm as she pulled. "Let go," he said. "We'll both go over."

"No."

Her tone was as uncompromising as the resolve in her eyes.

"Now brace your feet and walk up the side of the cliff." Was she joking? He was supposed to walk up a sheer wall of rock?

"Do it now." The Harper from six years ago would have tried to gently reason with him. This Harper barked out orders like an army sergeant.

He did as she said.

With shared determination, they managed to get him up and over the cliff edge. They lay side by side, panting together.

"Thanks," he said gruffly. She'd just saved his life, at the risk of her own. That was the Harper he remembered from six years ago, fearless and willing to take on anything. Anything but her father, who had ruled her with an iron fist.

Now wasn't the time to give way to harsh memories, memories that still had the power to sear his heart with regret.

She stood, extended a hand to him. "Let's go. Unless

you need to rest." The challenge in her voice was unmistakable. When he didn't respond, she said, "Put your feet where I put mine."

Fifteen minutes later, they had traversed the rocky rim and were once more on solid ground.

They kept at it for another hour. "Time for a rest," she announced.

They stopped in a copse of trees that provided a measure of shelter from the wind. She pulled out roast beef sandwiches on thick homemade bread, apples and trail mix.

He eyed the feast with appreciation. "You packed enough for an army."

"Cold and wind make a person hungrier than usual," she said.

"So I've heard."

She flushed. "Of course, you knew that. You are a ranger, after all."

"Hey, I didn't mean it like that. You're exactly right. Cold and wind do make a person hungry." To prove his point, he bit into a sandwich and chewed with appreciation. He put away two sandwiches and an apple in record time.

After policing the area, they each made a trip into the brush to take care of business.

"I figure we have about four more hours of daylight," she said when she returned.

Luca nodded. If they pushed it anymore, they'd lose the light, and though traveling in the dark had its advantages, it also had its share of dangers. Better to stop and then get an early start in the morning.

He thought about the instructions Harper had been given. Trade drugs for their son's life. As much as he yearned to get back the son he'd never seen, he couldn't be party to putting more drugs on the street.

Like a ruptured appendix, the drug trade had exploded. That the explosion had occurred decades ago made no difference in its effects on the country. Families were still being destroyed. Babies born to crack-addicted mothers still faced a lifetime of problems.

Drugs were no respecter of persons. They attacked the young and old, the rich and poor, the fortunate and unfortunate alike. There was no way he could return this poison to those who dealt in the trade. At the same time, he had to rescue his son.

His son.

The two words swirled in his mind. He was at once eager to meet the boy whom he'd fathered and terrified that he wouldn't measure up as a father. What made him think that he knew anything about being a father? His own father had been the worst possible model, a man who had freely used his fists and belt to beat some sense into the young Luca.

No way would he ever subject a child to that brand of parenting.

Neither he nor Harper had been winners in the parent lottery, he reflected. Her mother had died early while his had skipped out before he'd turned five. Harper knew his desire for a real family and his resolve to be the kind of father he'd never had. How could she have kept his son from him?

Impatient with himself for dredging up the past yet again, he did his best to shake off the feelings. His mission was to rescue Danny.

What he would give to have a few of his ranger buddies with him. They would know how to *persuade* the men who took Danny.

"Before we do anything, we have to find the drugs. That gives us a bargaining chip." He looked at her keenly. "You know we can't let them have the drugs. Hundreds, maybe thousands, of lives will be destroyed if those make it to the street."

She drew herself up. "Danny comes first." When she shuddered, he knew it wasn't solely due to the cold.

"When this is over, we're going to have a talk," he said as he readied to resume their trek. "A long talk."

She visibly shrank at his tone. "Let's get Danny back, and then you can rake me over the coals if that's what you need to do."

What she said made sense. It was too bad that he wasn't in the mood for things that made sense. In less than twenty-four hours, he'd learned that he had a son and that that son had been kidnapped.

Harper shifted as the straps of the knapsack dug into her shoulders.

Except for the few exchanged words when they'd stopped to eat, Luca was curt to the point of rudeness. Minutes dragged into hours as they remained locked in their own thoughts during their hike up the mountain. Fear and guilt swirled through her mind. While she was rescuing another child, her child had been taken.

As an independent search-and-rescue specialist, she'd received a call about a boy missing in the mountains. Finding the lost child had been the reward for returning home exhausted and nearly frozen, only to find her own son missing.

She tucked the guilt away and focused on the here and now.

The higher they climbed, the colder the temperature, their breath coming in plumes of frigid air. When she asked Luca how he was doing, he limited his answers to a grunt. The day promised to be even longer as the tension between them grew. She wanted to tell him about Danny, about what a great boy he was, but the thick air between them kept the words unsaid.

The Luca she remembered was slow to anger. She didn't know this Luca. He was an explosion waiting to happen.

She knew he was furious with her and didn't blame him. From his perspective, she'd kept his son from him for five years. Apparently, the letters she'd written to Luca, the pictures of Danny she'd sent, didn't count.

She tried once more. "I know you're angry, but—"

"Don't," he said, cutting her off. "Just…don't."

"We need to work together. We can't do that unless we talk. And we can't talk, really talk, until you say what it is you have to say."

"How am I supposed to get over learning that you kept my son from me for five years? *Five years*." He scrubbed a gloved hand over his face. "Do you know what that feels like? You know what my father was like. Is that why you didn't tell me? Because you were afraid I'd end up being like him?"

Harper heard the frustration in his voice and read the pain in his eyes. She recalled what he'd told her of his own childhood and how he wanted to give his children the love he had never received. "It was never that. Never." She drew a shaky breath. "Can we focus on getting our son back?"

"So now he's *our* son?"

"He was always our son."

"Thanks for that." Sarcasm hung heavy.

She put out a hand. "Luca, please."

He ignored the peace offering and shifted his gaze so that it landed anywhere but on her. She knew Luca wasn't finished with his anger. He blamed her for keeping Danny from him. Fine by her. There was plenty of blame to go round.

Why was it fair for him to be all over her when he hadn't

owned up to his part in the heartache they'd both suffered? Should she ask him why he'd never responded to the letters and pictures she'd sent him following Danny's birth? There'd be time—later—to sort things out, but time was running out for Danny and Vera.

She struggled to call a halt. It wasn't hard to see that Luca felt the same. But they were running out of daylight. Few words were spoken as she and Luca set up camp. They operated as a team, each anticipating what needed to be done. She snuck a few glances at him, trying to read his body language but failing.

Dinner was simple but hearty fare. She dug through her knapsack and came away with hotdogs, which they cooked over a fire, cans of beans and more apples, with oversized candy bars for dessert.

"I see you're determined to keep the doctor away," he said, pointing to the apples.

"What? Yeah. I guess." Her expression dismal, she said, "You know they're not going to just give Danny and Vera back to us." Tears ran down her cheeks, hot and thin. She didn't bother wiping them away. They were proof that she was still functioning. If Luca saw them as weaknesses, she couldn't worry over it.

But the expression in his eyes was one of compassion, and she chastised herself for thinking he'd condemn her for a few tears. That wasn't who he was. He was strong and courageous, yes, yet also kind and compassionate.

Despite the circumstances they found themselves in, she spared a moment to study him. The rugged cast of his features spoke of a man who had known pain, yet it didn't distract from his appeal. His face, always lean, had been boyishly handsome, but it was now defined by hard lines of determination. His body had filled out with muscle and sinew. There was an inherent strength to him that said that while he might bend, he would never break.

He didn't say anything, only reached for her hand and squeezed it briefly. This was the Luca she remembered. During their courtship, he'd listened while she'd spilled out her feelings about her father and his petty cruelties. He'd held her when she'd cried and then gently wiped away the tears with his thumbs. He'd stroked her hair and promised that their life together would be one of love.

If only she'd stood up to her father. If only she'd had the strength to do what was right. If only.

The words echoed in her mind as she slept fitfully then woke early. After they choked down a breakfast of bread toasted over the fire and coffee, they cleaned up their campsite and set out.

After a few hours following her calculations on where the wind would likely have carried the package, they found it.

She was good at her job. No brag, just fact. Starting a search-and-rescue business hadn't been her goal; she'd fallen into it when a neighbor's child had gone missing. The whole town had turned out to find the little girl, but it had been Harper who had tracked the tiny footprints and followed them until they had ended at an abandoned mine shaft. It had been her who had discovered the child on a ledge of the shaft and pulled her out. From then on, she'd become the go-to person when someone was lost or missing, especially a child.

She switched her thoughts to the problem of recovering the drugs. The package had fallen to the base of a large crevice in a rocky area. There was no way to reach it except to scale the wall of sheer rock, made more treacherous with a fine coating of ice.

"I'll go," Luca said.

She shook her head. "There are no hand or footholds. One of us has to lower the other down."

Her search-and-rescue efforts had taught her how to negotiate a cliff. Success depended upon having a partner with enough strength to pull her back up. As he outweighed her by eighty pounds or more, she would have to be the one to go after the drugs.

Grateful that she'd packed a harness, she slipped it over her shoulders and around her waist. She glanced down and inhaled a deep breath. *Suck it up, buttercup.*

The first part went easily enough, and she made it quickly to a ledge in the crevasse. But when she couldn't reach the package of drugs from where she was, she called to Luca, "Swing me over."

He gave the rope a hard rock to the left, and, after two tries, she was still unable to reach the package.

"Again," she called up to him.

He swung the rope, harder this time. Unable to stop its momentum, she hit the rock face, rapping her head hard. At the same time, she felt the harness snap under the strain. Suspended over a deep crevasse, she realized she was without a safety net.

Dizziness churned through her. She clamped down on it; she couldn't afford to pass out. She found purchase on the small ledge once again. She just needed to get her breath. That was all.

"Harper." Luca's voice was sharp. "Are you all right?"

"Y-yeah." But her voice told a different story.

"I'm coming down," he called.

"You can't. You have to pull me up." Unspoken was the acknowledgment that he struggled with heights.

"Give me a minute to anchor the rope."

"Luca, no." But she was too late. He'd already stepped away.

Her breathing was becoming shallow, and she knew she was on the verge of giving into the light-headedness caused by hitting her head. Then she saw Luca descending into the crevasse.

When he reached her, she slumped against him. "Steady," he said. "I'm going to reach around you and get the package, and then we're going to climb up." Kicking off the rock wall, he swung past her and got his fingertips on the package on the second try.

"The harness..." she said when he returned to her on the ledge.

"No problem. I'll carry you up. Put your arms around my neck and interlock your fingers. Wrap your legs around me."

She felt the bunching and tightening of his muscles as he strained to get them to the top of the cliff.

How he did it, she didn't know. When they reached safety, they fell to the ground and lay there.

Luca got to his knees and bent over her. "Let me see your head." He found the first aid kit in her pack and bandaged the scrape on her forehead. "You're going to have quite a lump there. Are you still dizzy?"

She shook her head.

"Would you admit it if you were?"

"Probably not." She stood. "We can't afford to waste any more time."

With his knife, he slit the package open. Neither was surprised to find it filled with four bricks of cocaine. Enough supply to keep Colorado's youth in cocaine for weeks. It was no secret that high-school kids were being targeted, along with middle-school and grade-school kids.

Her lips thinned in anger. What kind of animals sold this poison to children?

Luca pulled a package of dried milk from his backpack and substituted it for the cocaine. Of similar consistency and weight, the powdered milk would buy them some time. He tucked the drugs in his pack.

"Now for the hard part," she said. With the drugs in her and Luca's possession, she sent a text to the number she'd been given.

Have drugs. Where is my son?

Coordinates came back of where to make the exchange. A mirthless smile touched her lips at the word. She wasn't so naïve to believe that the drug runners would hand over Danny and Vera just like that.

The hike to the location took less than an hour. She and Luca approached the spot from the north side and found a crudely set up camp, as though those inhabiting it expected to be there for only a short time.

Harper took her time and scoped out the grouping of tents. Rushing into a drug dealers' camp was a fool's move. She and Luca set a ring of small fires around the camp. She didn't worry about the fires spreading, not with all the snow, but the fires would serve as a distraction.

She had already considered their next move. "They don't expect anyone to be with me. I'll go in and keep their attention on me, while you find Danny and Vera. You'll have to move fast. They're going to figure out you switched powdered milk for the cocaine pretty quickly."

"You expect me to let you just stroll into the camp without any backup?"

"I expect you to do whatever you have to to save our son." Before he could stop her, she set off.

With every bit of courage she possessed, she walked

into the camp, holding the package. "I've got your drugs. I want my son."

A short man pushed his way forward. From the deferential way the other men stepped aside, she guessed that he was the boss. "Show me the drugs."

"Take me to my son."

Two men appeared at her sides and roughly grabbed her arms. One snatched the package from her and slit it open. After touching the knife into the powder, he took a small taste, then spat it on the ground. "Nothing but powdered milk."

"Did you think to fool me?" the man she'd pegged as the boss asked.

"No. I have the drugs. They're tucked away somewhere safe. But I want to see my son first. Then I'll bring them to you."

A man rushed forward. "*Jefe*, there are fires around us."

Jefe. Chief. She'd been right in pegging the shorter man as the boss.

"You are playing a dangerous game." Though he had not raised his voice, there was a hard cast to his mouth, along with a cruel gleam in his eyes. This was a man who enjoyed inflicting pain upon others.

He backhanded her, sending her to the snow-packed ground. The impact worsened her already throbbing headache.

"I'm not playing." She stood, wiped blood from her mouth and aimed a level gaze at him. As long as Danny was safe, she could take whatever came next.

She flexed her fingers and then curled them into fists. She was ready.

THREE

Lying prone on the freezing ground, Luca watched and listened as a couple of guards talked between themselves. He stiffened when he recognized the dialect they spoke, one he'd picked up while serving in Afghanistan when his unit had been assigned to bring down a terrorist cell.

It wasn't unheard of for terrorists to join forces with drug runners. It had proven a profitable union for both sides.

Luca had witnessed such partnerships in Afghanistan, where drug lords and terrorists aided and abetted each other. The exchange of drugs and money was one of the primary businesses in the country, preying on the weakness and desperation of people who had seen too much war and destruction over the last six decades.

Luca pulled his thoughts out of the past and concentrated on the now. From his years with the military, he knew watching and listening made up about three-quarters of any mission. Being able to remain totally still and entirely focused on a target for an interminable length of time had saved his life more than once.

He watched the guards. Dressed in black with body armor and carrying sub guns with a thirty-round extended mag, the men each took a drag on their smokes. Walkie-talkies attached to their shirtfronts enabled them to hear instructions.

A few minutes later, the men's conversation turned to Danny, and Luca learned that the cartel members had no intention of releasing him, even after they got their drugs. Most soldiers, whatever side they fought on, had an unwritten code that wives and children were to be left alone. These men had no such code and would exact their vengeance with pitiless cruelty.

He listened further and learned that his son was in the tent closest to the central one. Was Vera there, too? There'd been no mention of her. After the guards moved on, Luca made his way to the back side of the tent, crawling under the reinforced nylon. The boy's hands and feet were tied together, making him look like a turkey trussed up for Thanksgiving dinner. A gag was stuffed in his mouth.

His son.

Luca grimaced at the sight as fury roiled through him. He did his best to tamp it down. Right now, he needed to focus on getting Danny out of here, but later whoever did this would pay. They would pay big time. He removed the gag and put a finger to Danny's lips, signaling him not to speak. His eyes full of questions, the boy nodded.

Luca looked about for Vera, but there was no sign of her. Nor had he seen men guarding a second tent, indicating a prisoner was being held there, on his way in.

Fortunately, Danny's coat had been tossed in a corner. With his arms and hands numb from being bound, he was unable to get them into the sleeves of the coat, and Luca helped him.

"Have you seen Vera?" Luca whispered.

Danny shook his head. "They took her away." His lips trembled. "She was crying."

Luca processed that. He couldn't afford to search for the housekeeper now, not if he were to get Danny to safety. "Can you walk?" he asked.

Danny took a few tentative steps. His legs were in no better shape than his arms and hands. Luca scooped him into his arms. "I need you to wrap your arms around my neck. Can you do that?"

At Danny's nod, Luca switched him to his back, so that he rode piggy-back style.

They made good on their getaway until Danny shouted, "It's Mommy. She's in trouble."

Luca followed Danny's gaze and watched as Harper was held captive by two men. "Mommy!" Danny's shout caused Luca to pause.

"Keep going," she yelled. "Keep going."

Luca winced when one of the men clipped her on the jaw, knocking her to the ground.

"Get Danny out of here," she shouted.

Danny beat on Luca's back. "That's my mommy. We need to help her."

"Your mother sent me to get you," Luca said. "I'll go back for her when I stash you somewhere safe."

"They're hurting her." A five-year-old boy should never have to say those words, especially regarding his mother.

Luca didn't answer the boy's plaintive cry. How could he? Nothing he could say would change what they had both witnessed.

Harper didn't try to fight. Not now. She'd save her strength for when it counted. For now, she would bide her time. Waiting had never been one of her strengths. She hoped the fires she and Luca had started would keep the men busy for a while, giving Luca more time to get Danny far away.

A man nearly as tall as Luca pushed her into a tent, sending her to the ground.

The smaller man—the boss—strode inside. "Allow me to introduce myself. I am your host. El Jefe."

Well-groomed and dressed, he appeared more civilized than the other men. "You set the fires. A clever distraction."

She remained silent.

"You are a brave woman. But also one who is lacking in intelligence. Did you think trading your life for your son's would keep him safe?"

She refused to react, though fear for Danny chased through her. Had Luca gotten him out? Were they even now on their way to the ranch? If Danny was all right, she could handle whatever happened to herself. And what about Vera?

The man crossed his arms over his chest. Suddenly, his lack of height didn't matter. The chill in his eyes promised that her next hours would be…uncomfortable. She wanted to laugh at the weak word. "You have nothing to say? That is unfortunate. You will be begging me to talk soon enough."

Fear traced a cold finger down her spine, but she refused to show it in front of these men, men who traded on the fear and pain of others. "I don't beg."

"We will see."

She thrust out her chin. "You're a real breath of stale air."

The other man guffawed, then thought better of it.

El Jefe pulled back his arm and punched her in the face, sending her to the ground for the second time. "You think you are funny. Your smart mouth will cause you more pain if you do not keep it shut."

With an effort she refused to allow him to see, she pushed herself up and faced him. She felt the blood trickling down her chin and onto her neck, but she didn't wipe it away, unwilling to give him that satisfaction.

"You will apologize."

"No."

He drew back his arm as though to hit her again but didn't carry through. "You will suffer enough later on." He turned to his second-in-command. "Take her away and lock her up."

"Should I give her food?"

"Of course. She will die soon enough. Let her have food now." He sent her a cruel smile. "See? I am not an unreasonable man."

She kept her mouth shut. Though he hadn't hit her again, there was no need to give him cause to change his mind. The punch to her face had loosened a couple of teeth and sent waves of pain through her jaw and down her neck. Her energy would be better spent coming up with a plan to get out of here. The prospects looked grim.

"Be grateful El Jefe did not decide to make an example out of you," the second-in-command said. "He does not like people who defy him. Especially women."

"I'll make a note of that."

The man frowned, obviously unsure of what to say. Finally, he left.

Harper searched the tent, looking for something, anything she could use as a weapon or to get out of here. Except for a cot and a bucket, there was nothing.

Think.

When the flaps to the tent opened, a young girl, probably no more than eighteen years old, entered, carrying a tray of food. "Senor Delgado says that you are to eat."

Harper didn't want to accept anything from the people who had kidnapped her son, but she recognized the wisdom of eating. She and Luca had been going hard for the last two days, and she needed the fuel for whatever came next.

She lifted the cloth covering the food and found tamales and rice. Would the men holding her have drugged it?

"It is okay," the girl said, apparently anticipating Harper's caution.

Too hungry to argue, Harper took a bite and found it, if not delicious, at least edible. "I have to get out of here," she said. "Will you help me?"

Torn between getting his son to safety and saving Harper, Luca hesitated. But only for a moment. Hesitation meant time wasted, and he couldn't afford that. With Danny wrapped around his chest now, he ran, zigzagging through the forest to avoid the barrage of bullets.

When he came to an area of thick brush, he stopped, looked for a hiding place and found one in a hollowed-out tree. It looked safe and snug. If he covered the opening with brush, it should go unnoticed by anyone looking for Danny.

Luca tucked his son inside the small space. "I've got to leave you while I go get your mom."

He could see the fear in Danny's eyes. The boy was only five, far too young to be left alone in the wilderness with armed men searching for him, but Luca didn't have a choice. Not if he wanted to get both Danny and Harper home safely. There had been no sign of Vera at the camp, and he reasoned that the kidnappers were keeping her in a different place, probably to make rescue that much more difficult. He'd have to come back for her.

"Bring my mommy back. Please."

The sniffle behind the words told Luca that Danny was making a valiant effort not to cry. *Brave boy.*

"I won't come back without her."

He had no right to say that. He wasn't given to making promises he wasn't certain he could keep. What if the men who held Harper decided to kill her in retaliation? He wouldn't put it past them.

"Whatever happens," he said, "stay here."

"What if I hear something?"

Luca knelt in front of his son. Searching for the right words, he said, "The only thing that matters is keeping you safe. If I know you're safe, then I can go get your mother. Does that make sense?"

Though Danny trembled in fear, he nodded.

Luca covered the opening of the hollow with fallen branches. He looked at his handiwork and decided it would do.

Now to find Harper.

He took a circuitous route back to the camp. It was a beehive of activity as men scrambled to put out the fires. The man who appeared to be the boss was shouting orders. Others scurried to obey.

Luca scanned the tents and looked for one that had a man or maybe two standing guard. That was where he would find her.

He spotted it easily. The first job was to distract the guard. That shouldn't be too difficult. He made a rustling noise at the back of the tent. The guard looked about but didn't leave his post.

Luca repeated the sound. This time, the guard cautiously approached the direction from which the sound came. When he came close enough, Luca gave him a swift chop to the neck, rendering him unconscious.

He dragged him into the bush and began stripping off the man's clothes. Fortunately, the man was twenty or so pounds heavier than Luca, so the clothes fit over Luca's own with little problem. Once he was dressed, he used flex-cuffs to bind the man's hands and feet. A kerchief stuffed in his mouth took care of any attempt to call out for help.

Harper huddled inside the tent. She was brutally cold. With her hands bound behind her now, she couldn't even cross her arms over her chest to warm herself.

When the flap to the tent was lifted, she steeled herself for what was to come and didn't look up. The intruder crossed the small space to her, and she braced herself, prepared to fight.

"Harper. It's me."

Luca?

"What are you doing here?" she demanded. "You're supposed to be getting Danny out of here."

"He's safe. He's some kid. Demanded that the two of us go back and get you."

"Is he all right?"

"He told me to bring you back, and that's what I'm going to do."

"What about Vera?" In her worry over Danny, she had almost forgotten about the housekeeper.

"I was hoping she was here with you. This is the only tent that has a guard in front. We'll come back and get her, but first we have to get Danny to safety."

"You know that we're surrounded by cartel members. They're not going to let you just waltz out of here with me."

"You're right. But if I pretend that I'm taking you to the woods for a bathroom break, they won't think anything about it."

Could they pull it off?

"Untie me," she said.

He loosened the bindings around her wrists but didn't remove them. "They'll expect you to be bound."

Outside the tent, he pushed her toward the woods, answering one of the men's questions with a crude word.

"As soon as we get out of sight, start running."

"What about you?"

"I'll be right behind you."

She didn't believe him. He was going to delay the men who would undoubtedly give chase.

"Let me have a weapon."

Before he could pull his sidepiece from his ankle holster, a commotion back at the camp alerted them that her absence had been discovered. Trampling in the snow ensued, telling her that their trail had been picked up.

"Run."

She ran for all she was worth, gratified to see that she hadn't lost her sprinting ability from when she'd been on the track team in high school. Luca followed.

Rifle shots pierced the air and strafed the ground. Something hit her in the shoulder, but she couldn't stop.

When the shooting came to a halt, Luca held up a hand in the air, the universal signal to stop.

She wasn't sorry to give her lungs and her legs a rest. "That was close."

"Too close." He closed his hands over her shoulders.

Frowning, he pulled his hands away, and she saw that they were dark, coated with a substance she couldn't immediately identify.

And then she knew. They were coated with blood. Her blood.

FOUR

"Harper." Luca's voice reached her ears, but she couldn't respond. "Harper," he repeated, more loudly this time. "You've been shot."

"I've been shot?" She remembered a hit to her shoulder as they ran from the camp, but the pain didn't fully register. It was as if she couldn't wrap her mind around it. She put a gloved hand to her shoulder, almost surprised when it came away bloody.

"Harper, can you walk?"

In answer, she tried a step. Another. Her legs were unsteady, and her knees threatened to buckle.

"Never mind," he said and scooped her into his arms.

"You can't carry me."

He didn't bother answering. He set out running through the deep snow.

Within ten minutes, they came to a secluded area surrounded by thickets. Luca cleared some brush from the front of an old, gnarled tree.

"Danny?" he called. "You can come out."

Danny emerged from a hollowed-out tree. "Mom?" His voice rose. "What happened?"

"I'm all right," she said, despite her promise never to lie

to her son. She was very much not all right, but she couldn't tell him that. Not after what he'd been through.

Luca stepped between them. "Danny, see that pack over there?" At his nod, Luca said, "Bring it here."

After the boy returned, Luca spread out the tarp he removed from the backpack and then carefully helped Harper to lie down on it. "I've got to see what we're dealing with," he said.

She nodded. "Go ahead."

He helped her out of her jacket and then carefully loosened her collar. Gently, he probed her shoulder. "The bullet's still in there."

She understood what he was saying. Infection could easily set in if the bullet were allowed to remain inside.

Luca had never been one to shirk his duty and would do what was necessary. She knew him well enough to understand that he'd rather have taken the bullet himself than remove one from her. He would be operating in primitive conditions, but what choice did they have?

"It's going to hurt, worse than getting shot itself," he said, his face pulled in grim lines. "We don't have any anesthesia."

"I can handle it." For good measure, she said it again. "I can handle it." If she said the words enough, she might start believing them. She was proud that her voice didn't tremble, as it might have.

Long seconds passed before he nodded. "We need to build a fire so that I can sterilize my knife."

She thought of the combat knife he carried. That was what he'd be using to dig out the bullet. She'd boasted that she could handle it, but could she? She'd endured having bones set, but this?

It didn't matter. The bullet had to come out.

"Mommy?" Danny's voice penetrated the quagmire of her thoughts.

"It'll be okay," she said, working to sound confident and unafraid. The truth was, she was terrified. She'd never been shot, much less had a bullet removed. Doing it in the middle of a snowstorm with bad guys chasing them took things to a new level. She trusted Luca, knew that he would do what was necessary to bring her through the ordeal.

"Mommy, are you sure?" Danny asked.

Unable to trust her voice, she nodded. She didn't want her son to know just how frightened she was.

With as much dispassion as she could muster, she watched as Luca set about building a small campfire. He unsheathed his knife and held it to the flames. She hadn't noticed before just how large the knife was, how deadly it looked. Well, what had she expected? It was a soldier's weapon, meant to take out an enemy. Now it would be used to take out a bullet. From her.

Could she stand up to the pain?

The answer came swiftly. She had to. But there was something she had to do first. "Danny," she said. "Would you do something for me?"

"Anything, Mommy."

"Would you go behind those trees over there?" She gestured to a stand of trees. They wouldn't block out everything, but they'd prevent him from seeing Luca operating on her. It was bad enough that she had to have a bullet taken out, but having her young son witness it would be worse. Much worse. She didn't want him to watch her suffer. *Dear Lord, please let me get through this without falling apart.* Danny had been kidnapped, held hostage and had fled from gunmen. He didn't need to see this.

"I want to help."

"I know," she said. "What will help me the most is if I know you don't have to see this. It's going to be…" She paused, searching for the right words. "It's going to be hard, and I don't want you to be hurt by it."

Resolve crossed his freckled face. "Okay."

"Thank you." She managed a smile. "Remember the stories we read about King Arthur and the Knights of the Round Table and how brave they were? That's what I need from you right now. To be brave. Can you do that for me?"

Danny nodded. "I can do it."

"That's my boy."

When he'd walked a short distance away, she turned to Luca. "Let's do this."

He pushed the neckline of her shirt aside. Blood-soaked cloth stuck to her skin, causing her to bite her lip. She refused to cry out. If she couldn't handle that, how was she to handle *real* pain?

Luca broke off a stick and gave her a small piece. "Bite down on this."

She'd seen cowboys do that in old Westerns. "I didn't know people really did this."

He gave her one last look. "Are you ready?"

"I'm ready." She tried for bravado and a smile. And failed miserably at both.

Luca's smile, probably meant to be encouraging, also failed to hit the mark.

She put the wood in her mouth and bit down.

"I have to find the bullet and then get it out," he warned, his voice suddenly hoarse. "It's not going to be easy."

Harper braced herself for the bite of the knife. As bad as she thought it would be, it was worse. Far worse.

Pain such as she'd never known ripped through her as

the heated steel seared her skin, but that was only the beginning. It grew worse as he began digging in her flesh.

"You're doing great," he said, but she wasn't paying attention.

She was too busy biting on the stick for all she was worth. Tears streamed down her face, but she refused to scream. They couldn't know if the drug runners were still searching for them, so she kept the scream inside.

"I've found it," he said. "Just a little more, and I'll have it."

But she didn't hear. She'd passed out.

When she fainted, it was a relief. Luca extracted the bullet and held it up to the fire. A 9 mm. Whoever had shot her had meant business. This was serious firepower.

One more chore to go. He would rather have taken a beating than put a knife to Harper's flesh again, but it had to be done. He heated the knife once more, then lay it flat against the wound, cauterizing it.

Her body bucked as the steel seared the flesh.

Having a white-hot knife pressed against an open wound under these rough-and-ready conditions was a test of valor. He'd known battle-hardened soldiers who had cried like a baby at the pain.

Danny ran to him and tried to pull his arm away. "Stop it. Stop it. You're hurting my mommy."

Luca shook him off as gently as possible. He couldn't afford a slip of the knife. "Do you want me to help your mom?"

"Yes."

"Then let me do this." Thirty more seconds should do it.

He counted down in his head then looked down to find that his hands were shaking. That was a first. He'd had the reputation among his ranger buddies for never reacting, much less flinching, but he'd done both when he'd put the knife to Harper's flesh.

From the first aid kit Harper had packed, he took a piece of sterile gauze and taped it over the wound.

His lips stretched into a grim line as he considered that the drug runners were likely searching for him, Harper and Danny. Cartel members weren't the kind to give up, especially when that much cocaine was involved.

He had to slow them down.

He leaned closer to Harper and whispered, "I'm going to backtrack, see if we picked up a tail." He didn't give her time to object. "I'll be back as soon as I can. You rest."

He left the Sig Sauer with Harper and tucked the Glock in the back of his waistband, though he preferred not to use it if it could be avoided. In the still mountain air, gunshots could be heard from miles around. If he needed a weapon, he hoped to make do with the K-Bar knife that he kept in his boot.

Melting into the forest, he retraced their steps, removing any signs that they had come this way. When he picked up on voices piercing the otherwise still night, he paused. Listened.

At least two men. Possibly three.

He removed his knife from his boot and held it in his right hand, concealing it behind his leg, then picked his way through the trees toward them. A single man hunkered down, studying something on the ground. He held a tactical flashlight. Two others gathered around him, rubbing their hands together.

Luca needed to take them out. Soundlessly, he approached them and circled his arm around the neck of one of the men standing. A quick twist of his arm sent the man to the ground. Before the others could react, he repeated the move on the man next to him. That left the man on the ground, who now stood, facing him, holding a Colt .45 on him.

"You will not find me so easy to take down," he said.

Luca didn't hesitate. He threw the knife, hitting his opponent squarely in the chest. A quick check told him that the man was dead. He felt no satisfaction in killing the man, but neither did he regret it.

Now he turned his attention to the other two. With quick efficiency, he bound their wrists with flex-cuffs and, after removing their boots, did the same with their ankles. He then searched them for weapons and tucked the guns in his belt. You never knew when extra firepower would come in handy.

He retraced his steps and arrived back where he'd left Harper and Danny less than an hour ago. With Harper wounded and the temperature well below zero, traveling was going to be anything but easy.

His lips compressed as he looked at the deep purple bruises around her neck. Someone had gone out of his way to hurt her. That was obvious. Luca would make certain that whoever had done it would pay and pay dearly for inflicting such pain on her.

Luca desperately needed rest, but he had to watch over Harper. Danny had fallen asleep beside her, his arm outstretched toward her, no doubt needing the presence of his mother despite her condition. Harper appeared to be resting easier. When she awoke, he slipped a couple of aspirins under her tongue and held a bottle of water to her lips.

She grunted her thanks, turned over and went back to sleep.

"Sleep," he whispered, even knowing she couldn't hear him. "Just sleep."

Luca was all too aware of their proximity. Did Harper feel it as well? Even if she did, it couldn't make a difference. He'd already decided there could be nothing between them and had erected a wall between them. If it weren't for the fact that she was wounded, he could almost be grateful for the extreme cold and the danger they faced from the drug runners who were most certainly after them.

It was better this way. Whatever had been between him and Harper had died six years ago. If that weren't enough, the knowledge that she'd deliberately kept his son from him had sealed the end of anything between them.

Several hours in, Harper stirred, her eyes opening. "Luca?"

"I'm here."

"Danny?"

"He's fine." The boy had curled up, his back now to them. Luca had wrapped them each in survival blankets he'd found in the first-aid kit. "You should try to get some more rest. We've got to hike out of here at first light."

"Can't sleep. Hurts too much. Talk to me. Maybe it'll take my mind off the pain."

"The bruises around your neck. How did you get them?"

Gingerly, she touched her throat where dark bruises marred the delicate skin. "The man who threatened me that first morning put a chokehold on me. He let up when he saw I was about to pass out."

Luca's lips tightened. "You didn't tell me that."

"You didn't give me the chance. You were too busy being angry with me."

"Okay. I deserve that. But you should have told me. I would have—"

"Would have what? There was nothing you could have done about it."

Just like there was nothing he could have done about his son. He tested the waters. "About Danny…" His eyes flicked toward the boy.

"What about him?"

"Why didn't you tell me about him? At least after he was born. I would have been there for you. For him."

He wanted to kick himself for bringing up the subject when she was weak and hurting, but it was too late now to snatch back the words.

"I did tell you, but you chose to ignore my letters." There was a snap to her voice that belied the paleness of her face.

Why had he let his mind take him down this path? This was clearly not the time nor the place for this discussion, but it was too late to pull back now, so he focused on what she'd just said.

"What letters?"

"The ones I sent you. I wrote as soon as I found out I was pregnant. I wrote every week during that first year. After Danny was born, I sent pictures until the Judge forced Danny and me to leave the ranch. When I didn't hear back from you, I figured you'd moved on."

"Do you honestly think I'd turn my back on my son?" Outrage and a good deal of hurt rimmed his voice, but he kept his voice low for fear of waking Danny.

How could she believe he would have deliberately ignored his child? She'd known about his family. A mother who had abandoned him and a father who had drunk himself to death. He'd vowed, if he ever had children of his own, that he would be the best parent he knew how to be.

"No. Not at first. But what was I supposed to think when a year passed, and I didn't hear one word from you? I kept waiting, hoping you'd write. But nothing ever came."

"I never received any letters." He'd joined the military

shortly after leaving Harper, but the military was good at forwarding mail. He tried to keep the accusation from his voice, but from her expression, he hadn't succeeded.

"That can't be. I sent dozens of letters until I accepted that you didn't want to know anything about Danny."

One of them was lying.

Harper saw the doubt in Luca's eyes. He didn't believe her. That hurt nearly as much as the wound in her shoulder. She wanted to lash out at him for his lack of trust, then stopped as the truth became clear. "The Judge."

"What about the Judge?"

"I always put my letters with the rest of the mail to go out. He took them to the city when he went to work, said they'd get to wherever they were going faster if they were mailed from there." How could she have been so foolish? Her father had never mailed the letters.

"And I suppose that you never received any letters from me," he said. There was no question in the words.

She shook her head. "You wrote to me?"

"Every week for that first year."

Once again, her father had stolen from her, this time the link to the man she'd loved with all her heart. "I don't know what to say."

A howl echoed through the night, interrupting her thoughts. It was followed by others, filling the silence, until a dozen pairs of yellow eyes pierced the darkness. Wolves, lean and hungry, circled the campsite. She'd expected it, knowing that the fierce winter had sent wolves, who normally avoided humans, to new territory in search of food.

She had come prepared. Her hand hovered over her weapon.

"They're closing in," Luca said.

"As long as we keep the fire going, we should be all right."

"'Should be'?"

"Yeah. Should be. Nothing's for certain. Not in the mountains."

After a while, the wolves, apparently sensing that their would-be meal wouldn't be easy pickings, took off, searching for other prey.

"I noticed you kept your hand on your weapon, but you never pulled it," Luca said.

"If I don't have to kill, I don't. The wolves are only trying to survive. Just like us."

"There hasn't been an *us* in six years," Luca pointed out.

"I'm telling you the truth," she said. "If you don't want to believe me, that's your choice."

She left him at that.

FIVE

Luca stayed awake long after Harper had once more slipped into sleep. He knew there wouldn't be any sleep for him. Aside from needing to make certain that neither the wolves nor the drug runners attacked, he wanted to make certain that her breathing was okay.

Something more, though, kept exhaustion from catching up to him. If she had been telling the truth about the letters she'd sent him—and he no longer had reason to doubt her—then everything he'd believed in the last six years had been a lie. He'd blamed her for not staying in touch with him. Understanding that it had been her father who had kept the truth from him eased his anger.

He'd thought he had a right to his grudge against her. Now he realized that she had been a victim of the Judge as much as he had. Maybe even more so. With her mother dead when Harper was just a child and only her father to raise her, she had received precious little love.

She'd been alone against a powerful man, her father no less. Alone and vulnerable. If Luca had been half the man he thought he was, he'd have gone back for her and convinced her to go away with him.

The Harper he remembered had never backed down from anything or anyone. Except one. Her father, Calvin Sloan, had her so thoroughly cowed that she couldn't see beyond the shadow he cast. And it was a long one.

The man had wielded power with the same heartlessness he'd meted out the harshest sentences in the Colorado court system. Mercy wasn't in his vocabulary. Only justice. He'd dispensed that with a heavy hand and a cold heart. Especially when it came to dealing with his daughter and only child.

Luca's lips twisted as he recalled finding Harper crying one afternoon after her father had beaten her with his belt. That was Big Cal's way. If he couldn't command her obedience, he beat it into her.

Luca made it a practice never to lie to himself. While deployed, he'd taken lives, more than he wanted to count. He didn't brag about it, but neither did he try to white-wash it. War had taken much from him, but he didn't regret the time he served. It had been an honor to serve and protect his country.

But he'd been lying to himself ever since he'd allowed the annulment to take place. He'd pretended that his feelings for Harper were over, that they'd died when she'd agreed to her father's demands.

Sometimes he'd even believed the lies, but deep down in his heart of hearts, he knew them for what they were. Loving her was so ingrained within him that he didn't know how to stop.

The truth was that he'd never stopped loving her.

For now, he was charged with protecting both her and their son. They would sort out the rest when the danger was over. He thought of how she'd sacrificed herself so that he could free Danny and then how she'd been ready to take on the wolves, even when wounded. She was as brave as any man with whom he'd worked. Only when her son was threatened had she shown fear.

Why had the cartel chosen Harper to find and retrieve the drugs? The question reared again in his mind and continued to nag at him.

There were other search-and-rescue specialists they could have used. Why her? Sure, she had a good rep, but so did others. And why kidnap Danny in the first place? Why not simply take Harper and force her to do the job? Taking Danny made it infinitely more difficult for the kidnappers. A hostage, even a child, had to be watched, guarded. Then there was the added complication of taking Vera.

Returning Danny had been presented as a trade. The cocaine for Danny. But something felt off about it. It was as if Harper had been targeted for reasons greater than simply retrieving the drugs. Someone had a grudge against her, one strong enough to threaten the most important person in her life: Danny. That was about as personal as it got.

Who would hate her that much?

It made no sense. No sense at all.

He tried different scenarios, but none of them fit. They felt forced, taking him back to his original question: why choose Harper? The question gnawed at him.

Why her?

He continued to mull it over until weariness he could no longer fight overtook him. When he woke, it was to find Danny staring at him.

Luca didn't want to scare his son. Danny had been through more than any child should. "Hey, Danny." He kept his voice low, so as not to disturb Harper.

The little boy regarded him gravely. "You brought my mommy back."

"That's right."

"The bad men tried to hurt her."

"I know. But we're not going to let them hurt you or her again."

"I was scared," Danny said, his lip trembling.

"You were right to be scared."

"Is Mommy going to be all right?"

"Yes." There he went again, making promises he wasn't certain he could keep. "We're going to take her to a hospital."

"Mommy took me to a hospital when I broke my arm. It's all better now."

"That's good. The doctors will make your mommy all better, too."

Danny leaned in and wrapped his arms around Luca's neck. "I think I like you."

Tears pricking his eyes, Luca hugged his son gently in return. "Thank you. I like you, too." The depth of his feelings reached inside of him and squeezed his heart. He had a son. Four small words that would forever define him.

Harper awoke, disoriented. Her mind was fuzzy. *Fuzzy and muzzy.* She wanted to laugh at the foolish rhyme. Hadn't she read a children's book with those very words to Danny a few years ago?

Pain dispelled the confusion. She'd been shot. Luca had removed the bullet. That much she was sure of. Had she dreamed the conversation about the letters?

She looked around, saw him hunkering over the campfire, warming his hands. After managing to sit up, she let out a chuff of pain. Where was Danny?

"He's right here," Luca said, guessing at her thoughts and gesturing to where Danny poked at the fire with a stick.

He poured a cup of coffee and brought it to her. "Careful. It's hot."

He was right. It was hot. It was also the most awful coffee she'd ever tasted, but it sent a much-welcomed stream of warmth through her, and she took another sip. "Thanks."

"Let's check your wound." After pushing aside her shirt collar, he examined her shoulder. "It hasn't bled through the bandages. That's a good sign." He hesitated. "About last night, I should never have brought up…what we talked about, not when you were hurting. I'm sorry."

"I'm not. Maybe we can forgive each other now that we know what happened."

Luca didn't respond. She didn't expect him to, but she'd hoped that at least some of the misunderstandings between them had been cleared up.

She forced that from her mind and thought of what came next. They would have to walk out of here. It was a long trek but doable. At least, it would have been if she hadn't been wounded. She set her jaw. A bullet to the shoulder wasn't going to stop her from getting her son to safety.

Mentally, she reviewed the few supplies she and Luca had left. Powdered eggs and coffee.

Danny scrambled over to her. "Mommy, are you okay?" His gaze searched her eyes, his young face drawn tight with lines of anxiety.

"I will be. Thanks to Luca."

From over by the campfire, Luca sent a smile their way then continued his task of melting snow for water to mix with the powdered eggs. When he handed her a plate of scrambled eggs, it was all she could do not to grimace at the sight of them. Knowing she needed protein, she geared herself up to eat them and managed to choke down a few bites.

"I know," he said. "Pretty awful, aren't they?"

"They're the awful-est eggs I've ever tasted," Danny said, holding his empty fork at his mouth.

"Danny," Harper admonished. "You know better."

"Sorry," he muttered.

"Danny's only telling the truth," Luca said. "The eggs are awful. But they're the only thing we have, and we're going to need fuel to make it back to the ranch."

She swallowed another mouthful of eggs. "They're not bad," she said to Luca.

"Something about faint praise," he murmured.

The three of them ate in tense silence. Danny had asked few questions. Until now. But she knew they were coming.

"Mommy, why did those bad men take me?" His gaze reflected confusion.

"They wanted to force me to find something for them."

"Did you?"

"Yes. But I didn't give it to them."

He nodded in satisfaction. "Good."

"How do you know it's good that she didn't?" Luca asked.

"Because if they kidnapped me and wanted my mom to find something for them, it had to be something bad."

"It was," Luca confirmed. "What do you know about drugs?"

"I know that they're not good for you." Danny made a face. "I'm glad you didn't help the bad men."

She was grateful to be able to confirm her son's good opinion of her, but she knew that she and Danny and Luca were far from safe. They'd obtained a temporary reprieve. That was all. She swallowed past the lump of fear that had taken up what felt like permanent residence in her throat.

Danny switched his attention and eyed Luca with a mix of hero worship and curiosity. "Who're you?"

She and Luca exchanged a look.

"I'm a friend of your mom's," Luca said at last. "I knew her from a long time ago. Before you were born."

"Did you come to help find me?"

"That's right."

Harper took up the story. "I knew I couldn't get you back on my own, so I asked Luca for help."

"You must be awfully brave," Danny said to Luca.

"Luca's plenty brave," Harper answered for him, knowing he had never been one given to bragging about himself. "He was an army ranger."

An uncomfortable look passed over Luca's face. "Eat your eggs, everyone. We need to get moving." He lowered his voice so that only Harper could hear him. "They'll be coming for us, and they'll be armed and hunting for bear."

Harper stood. "Haven't you heard about mama grizzlies? We'll fight to the death to protect our young."

She heard a rustling in the bushes. "There's someone—" Before she could get out the last word, two men jumped out at them.

"Thought you'd get away from us, didn't you?" one taunted.

Luca didn't give them time to act. He kicked the gun from one's hand, then clotheslined the other with his forearm, but the first man came at him, fists raised.

Harper winced as Luca took a fist to the jaw. He staggered but held his ground. She was always up for a challenge, but could she fight off trained combatants with her injury?

But she wasn't about to let Luca take on both men. After pushing Danny behind her, she jumped on one's back and beat against his head with her fists, clinging to him like a burr. She didn't delude herself into believing she could take him down, but maybe she could keep him from joining his compadre in battling Luca. Her hopes died when he flung her off.

His partner grabbed her wounded shoulder and spun her around. For one terrifying moment, she feared she would pass out as pain screamed through her.

Danny needs you. The reminder steadied her.

She struck out with her leg and caught him in the groin. The agony that filled his eyes gave her a moment's satisfaction.

With him out of commission, she grabbed the gun Luca had kicked from the first attacker's hand. Her grip on the weapon steady, she could and would use it if she had to. "Both of you, back off," she ordered.

"You think we're scared of a little thing like you?" the man asked, a feral look in his eyes. "I could eat you for breakfast in one bite."

She fired, narrowly missing his feet on purpose and causing him to dance to the side.

"You want to rethink that?" Luca asked. "Good work," he said to Harper.

Danny ran to her and grabbed her around the waist. "You were awesome, Mommy."

She didn't feel awesome. In fact, she felt pretty awful. Her shoulder and arm ached, making her wonder how she was going to hike out of here. She pulled up a smile for her son. She couldn't let him know how truly bad off she was. He'd had enough to deal with over the last two days.

"Keep the gun on them while I tie them up," Luca told her.

"No problem." She put as much energy in her voice as she could summon and resisted the urge to dart another glance at Danny. How was he holding up during all of this? Despite his brave front, he was still a little boy.

Quickly and efficiently, Luca pulled flex-cuffs from his pocket and bound the men's hands. He unthreaded their belts and used them to shackle their feet. "That should keep them. These two didn't come here alone," he said. "We have to move. Now."

Harper knelt to remove the men's boots. "They won't be going far."

Luca grinned. "I like the way you think."

"You can't leave us here," one of the men whined.

"Watch us," Luca said. "You'll work your way free soon enough, and then, if you know what's good for you, you'll head back the way you came. You don't have supplies. If you keep tracking us, you'll end up stuck out here in the night with no food, no tent, nothing to keep the cold out. Or the wolves away.

"One more thing." He searched first one man and then the other and came away with a set of keys.

Harper gave silent thanks that the men hadn't been able to take them prisoner, but she was hurting in earnest now. The adrenaline rush that had sustained her through taking down the men who'd attacked them had now subsided.

Can't be helped. Deal with it.

With the two men safely bound and gagged, Luca searched for their vehicle. He doubted they had walked far. To his relief, he found a Jeep parked a short distance away. His relief, though, was tempered with a large dose of worry.

Harper was in a bad way. He saw it in the white lines bracketing her mouth and the determined set to her jaw. He knew she wouldn't say anything. That wasn't who she was.

She'd grown into a beautiful woman as he'd known she

would, but there was a tensile strength to her now that hadn't been there six years ago. The Judge had cost them so many years, years they could have had together. Years where he could have watched his son grow up. Years where he and Harper could have grown more and more in love with each other.

Enough.

Flipping a mental switch, he steered away from the minefields of what could have been and refocused his thoughts on the very real danger of the present. He had to get Harper medical attention. Oh, and by the way, he had to avoid the cartel members who were intent on killing her, Danny and him.

Within a few minutes, they were loaded in the Jeep and on their way. When he heard her wince as the vehicle bumped over a rough spot in the road, his worry intensified. She needed to get to the hospital right away, and they were at least two hours—two long hours—from town.

He pressed down on the pedal fractionally harder, doing his best to balance speed with safety. Within the next hour, they should reach a main road.

He saw the concern in Harper's eyes and knew it was for their son, not for herself. Danny had said very little since they'd left their camp. What had he seen and heard? How much had he internalized?

"Are you all right, Danny?" she asked.

"Sure. I was sort of scared at first, but you and Luca took care of the bad guys. It was the coolest thing ever."

Luca suppressed a grin over the dismay in Harper's eyes. Like most mothers, she didn't want her child to be exposed to violence. He agreed to an extent, but he, more than most, knew that violence existed. They couldn't wrap Danny in cotton, hoping to keep him naïve about the world's ugliness.

The thought gave him pause. Without even thinking about it, he was inserting himself in Danny's future, giving himself a place in his son's life. What that place would look like, he didn't know. He only knew that he couldn't walk out of Danny's life now, but neither could he take him from Harper.

He didn't know how the three of them would work it out, but he refused to be cut out of the picture any longer.

Danny turned his attention toward Luca. "You sure showed them. You weren't scared one bit."

"I was plenty scared," Luca contradicted, meeting the boy's gaze in the rearview mirror.

Some of the light in Danny's eyes died, his disappointment palpable. "You didn't look scared."

"I was scared all right," Luca repeated. "Scared for you and your mom and me."

"But you beat them. Isn't that what counts?" The hero worship on Danny's face had faded.

Luca heard the puzzlement in his son's voice and did his best to answer in words a five-year-old could understand.

"We don't go around looking for fights," he said carefully, "but sometimes they're forced upon us, and we have to be ready. Men like the ones back there don't play fair. They want something so badly that they're willing to do anything to get it."

"Things like hurting my mom?" The quiver in Danny's voice betrayed his fear for his mother.

Luca didn't want to add to his son's fear, but he wouldn't lie to him. "That's right. Things like hurting your mom."

Satisfied that he'd given Danny something to think about, Luca kept his eyes on the road, which was hardly more than a goat track as it meandered its way east. He couldn't afford to let down his guard. They were still vulnerable to storms, mudslides, or fallen boulders. It wasn't nature's fury that he feared, though.

It was man's.

"So far, so good," Harper said, and he knew her thoughts had followed the same path his had, hoping that the drug dealers didn't have any more surprises in store for them before they reached town.

Within a few minutes, Danny had fallen asleep. She turned in her seat and spread a blanket she'd found there over him.

"He's a terrific kid," Luca said. "You've done a good job raising him."

Pleasure and surprise crossed her face. "Thank you. But I didn't have much to do with it. He just instinctively does what's right. He hasn't always had an easy time of it, but he never complains." A faint smile touched her lips. "At least, hardly ever."

Luca returned the smile with one of his own. "I can see you in him."

"And you," she added softly.

"What did the old man think of him?"

Her brow puckered at the same time her smile died. "The Judge kicked me out after Danny was born when I refused to give him up for adoption."

Luca had always known that her father was a snake, cold and heartless, but to order his daughter to give up her child? That took meanness to a new low.

"What did you do?"

"I took Danny and moved to the city. I went back to school and took a class in coding. I found a job where I could work from home. Things were tight for a while," she said with a wry laugh. "We lived on ramen and not much else. When Danny started preschool, I worked more hours. There wasn't much money for extras, but we made do."

"The Judge cut you off completely?" When she didn't respond, he guessed at the answer. "It was because of me, wasn't it? He didn't want *my* child anywhere near him."

"The great Calvin Sloan never had anything for me but the back of his hand."

"If he felt like he did about Danny, why did he leave him the ranch?"

"I think when he realized he was dying, he regretted what he'd done and wanted to make it up to his grandson. It was his loss. He missed out on knowing what a truly great boy Danny is."

"That doesn't sound like the Judge."

She shrugged. "No, it doesn't." Regret moved into her eyes. "In the end, though, I was sorry for him. He was old and bitter and alone. He could have had Danny in his life for five years, but he chose to throw him away."

"Just like he did with you."

Her nod was abrupt. "Just like."

Luca didn't pursue the conversation. He could tell it caused her pain to remember the relationship she'd had with the Judge. If the man had lived a couple of centuries ago, he would doubtless have been known as a hanging judge. As it was, he'd had to content himself passing down the harshest sentences allowed by law. He was no less merciless with his only child.

If only…

The words ran through Luca's mind with relentless persistence. If only he'd been there to take care of mother and son. If only he hadn't turned tail and run. If only he'd been patient with Harper and helped her realize that they belonged together, no matter what the Judge said about it.

Instead, he'd all but ordered Harper to come with him. No wonder she'd refused. She'd suffered the Judge's orders for all of her life. She didn't need the man who claimed to love her issuing orders to her as well.

Her dad had always hated Luca because Luca refused to bow down in his presence. Things had escalated when Luca and Harper had started dating seriously.

But regret didn't change what couldn't be changed. It was time he remembered that. He'd keep Harper and Danny safe for now, but after that…he didn't know.

A blast of snow from behind told him that they were no longer alone on the road. Though it could be thrill-seekers out on an adventure, he feared it was something more sinister.

The Jeep held its own, but the pickup behind them was gathering momentum and closing the distance between them with alarming speed. He made out two men in the front seat. One man leaned out the passenger-side window and fired at them.

"Keep down," he shouted.

After making sure that a now awake Danny heeded the command, Harper ducked her head.

When the truck rammed them, Luca did his best to hold the Jeep steady, but the impact and the icy road sent it swerving. He righted the Jeep before it slid into the ditch. If he allowed that to happen, he doubted he'd be able to get it out, and would be at the mercy of the pickup driver and his sidekick and whoever was in the crew seat of the truck. There was no question that the men were heavily armed.

He saw Harper brace herself for a second hit.

"What are we going to do?" Her voice was calm, but he knew she understood the consequences if the men chasing them caught up with them.

Men like that would show no mercy, not even to a wounded woman and a young boy. They'd already proven just how far they were willing to go to retrieve the drugs.

"We're going to outrun them. If we can't do that, we'll think of something else."

Just what that something else would look like, he had no idea.

SIX

It wasn't in Harper to sit back and do nothing. "Give me your gun," she said.

Luca handed over his Sig. "Think you can take out the engine?"

"I'll do you one better than that." Despite the pain that had settled in her shoulder and arm, she knew she could do this. What was more, she *had* to do it.

Her father had been a truly terrible parent, but the one thing he'd done for her was to teach her how to shoot. She had refused to hunt game—the very idea of killing animals was abhorrent to her. Her refusal had been met with ridicule. But she had become an expert marksman. She'd won shooting contests all over the West and was just as good with her left hand as she was with her right, a piece of good fortune since her right arm was currently too painful.

She leaned out the window, took aim and shot out the right front tire of the truck chasing them. In case their pursuers had a spare, she shot the left one as well. With the front tires out of commission, the pickup ground to a shuddering stop. Shooting out tires wasn't nearly as easy as it was made out to be on television and in movies, but it was possible.

When she turned back to Luca, she couldn't help a grin of pride.

"Show-off. I knew you were good; I just didn't know just how good."

"Thanks." Adrenaline pumped through her at the victory, but she didn't deceive herself into thinking that the danger was over.

"That should keep them off our tails, at least for a while," he said. "Unless they have backup."

That deflated much of her sense of triumph. The men could easily contact someone to intercept them farther down the road. This was a well-equipped bunch who had made it clear they'd do anything to get their drugs back. It wasn't inconceivable that they would have more men ready to step in if these guys failed.

The cost of twisting and steadying her shooting hand was making itself known now that the adrenaline rush was over, and the throbbing in her shoulder had returned with a vengeance, morphing into a constant stabbing. Luca had done a good job sewing her up, but that didn't stop the ache from shooting down her arm in unrelenting waves of pain.

"You okay?" he asked.

"Yeah."

"Liar."

"Okay, so maybe I'm not a hundred percent, but I'll get through." There was no other choice. When her father had kicked her and Danny out of the only home she'd ever known, she'd pulled herself together and done what had to be done. She'd do the same now.

She didn't have a choice. If more bad guys came at them, she was prepared to do what was necessary. Protecting her son was everything, even if it meant killing. She called upon wells of strength she didn't know she possessed and promised herself that no one would ever lay hands on Danny again.

"Like I said before, you'd make a good ranger."

"Thanks." Was Luca starting to forgive her? She wasn't given time to ponder it when three snowmobiles encircled them. Special tracks on their skids made it possible for them to navigate the snow-packed road. How many men had the drug dealers sent after them?

"Danny, get down on the floor," Luca ordered. "You too, Harper."

No way was she going to leave the fight to him. Glass shattered as a bullet hit the window. She made certain her child was safe and covered and then picked up the gun.

"Mommy, I'm scared," Danny said, a whimper in his voice. He'd been brave for so long, but he was only a little boy.

"It'll be all right," she said, her voice stronger as anger at the men who'd abducted him and frightened him surged through her.

Snowmobiles swarmed around the Jeep like giant bees on steroids. They darted back and forth, doing their best to run the Jeep off the road. High-powered rifles were strapped to the drivers' backs. She knew exactly how many bullets were left in the Glock but she counted anyway. Three. Three shots left. Could she take them out?

There was only one way to find out.

Luca knew if the snowmobiles succeeded in running the Jeep off the road, he and Harper and Danny were finished. There was no way they could fight off three heavily armed men. Harper was a crack shot, but she didn't have the ammunition to take out the three men; plus, she was wounded.

How many men did the enemy have? He and Harper had

fought off two at the campsite. He'd counted two more in the pickup and now these three. They were outmanned and outgunned. What was more, they had Danny to think of. A stray bullet could easily hit him.

Luca shuddered at the idea of his son being shot. Memories of children killed in Afghanistan crowded his mind while goosebumps borne of fury prickled his skin. He gripped the steering wheel so tightly he feared he'd snap it in half.

He plowed into the snowmobile that was threatening to derail the Jeep, sending its driver flying. One down, two to go.

Harper repositioned herself and took aim.

"I told you to stay down."

"Shut up and drive. And try to keep us on the road."

She took out another driver. Her second shot missed the remaining driver. Luca had already done the math. One shot left.

Lines of pain bracketed her mouth, reminding him that she was in no shape to take on more tangos, but she had stepped up without hesitation. He'd always known that she was strong; now, he realized that he'd underestimated her. She was ferocious when it came to protecting her child.

They couldn't depend on Harper taking him out, so he rammed the Jeep into the remaining snowmobile. So hard was the thrust that the man went tumbling head over heels to land in a heap in a snowbank. The snowmobile careened in the opposite direction.

For a second, Luca considered stopping the truck and checking the three men to see if they carried any ID or phones, anything that would point him to their bosses. He rejected the idea as soon as it had formed, though. Pros like these wouldn't carry any identifying objects; besides, getting Harper to the hospital came first.

Harper slumped against the door, her face paler than it had been only minutes ago. She needed antibiotics, and, unless he missed his guess, a blood transfusion. He pressed harder on the accelerator pedal. If he'd still believed in prayer, he would have sent one heavenward right along now.

But prayer was no longer part of his life.

Rubbing her eyes, Harper straightened, looked around and saw that they were close to town. "How long have I been asleep?"

"Almost an hour."

She turned to check on Danny.

Despite the circumstances, he gave her a wide grin. "You snore, Mommy."

"Your mom was extra tired," Luca said. "That tends to make a person snore."

She turned back to Luca. "Thanks for that." She stretched. "Have you two been getting to know each other?"

"I told Luca about getting into a fight with Busby at school."

She recalled the incident where she'd been summoned to the school by the principal and read the riot act about fighting. She didn't like the idea of Danny fighting, but neither was she going to punish him for standing up to a bully. When she'd told the principal just that, he'd frowned but let it go.

"Were you bragging about it?" she asked, her voice tart as a green apple.

"Course not." After a long pause, Danny shot her a guilty look in the mirror. "Well, not much. Luca and I got it all straightened out."

"I'm glad to hear that."

"I like Luca. A lot."

So do I.

She had no claim on him, not anymore, but she couldn't prevent the warmth that settled in her heart whenever she looked at him. Be careful, she warned herself. She couldn't afford to let him get too close. And what would happen now that Luca knew about Danny?

"We talked about when it's okay to fight and when it's not," her son continued. "I told him that I was standing up for a little kid who was being picked on by a bigger one."

"And what did Luca say?"

"He said that if I couldn't make the bigger kid stop bullying the smaller one, it was all right if I socked him in the nose."

Luca winced. "I didn't put it exactly that way."

Harper raised a brow. "Oh? How did you put it?"

"I said it was like the United States stepping in to help a country that was being invaded by a larger force. Sometimes, you just have to say 'enough' and stand up for what's right."

"Luca's right," she said, earning surprised glances from both father and son. "Sometimes, you have to say 'enough.'"

"Luca's pretty smart," Danny decided.

"Yes, he is." She aimed an appreciative look in his direction. "I'm glad he's on our side."

"Me, too."

It was obvious that Luca had won Danny over. Had it only been three days since she'd gone to him for help?

Being shot at, chased by killers and nearly freezing to death tended to make the days and nights go by quickly.

"How are you feeling?" he asked.

"Not bad."

The skeptical look sent in her direction had her ducking her head. She'd never been able to lie effectively, and this one was a whopper. She was far from fine. Her forehead was hot to the touch, and she felt feverish.

"I'm okay. Really."

"You're so pale that I can practically see through you."

"I have Danny to see to," she said in a last-ditch attempt to get out of going to the hospital. "I can't leave him alone."

"I'll look after Danny."

Seeing that she wasn't going to win this fight, she slumped back against the seat and did her best to keep her eyes open. She must have fallen asleep again because when she next opened her eyes, she saw the bright lights of a medical center.

Though she'd protested going to the hospital, in truth, she was grateful to be there. The throbbing pain in her shoulder wouldn't quit.

"Let us see to her," she heard an attendant say to Luca when he took her inside and explained what had happened.

Danny's voice reached her from a distance. Distressed. "Mommy…"

"It'll be okay," she said.

Luca would take care of their son. With that thought, she let the orderlies take her away.

They had survived, but she knew it was far from over.

To her displeasure, the doctor who examined her said she'd need to be admitted. She made sure Danny was checked out as well and felt relief when he was pronounced "in good shape."

"Maybe you and Danny can find a motel room close by. You have to be exhausted, and I know Danny is," she said to Luca when she'd been settled into a room.

"Danny and I aren't going anywhere. We're going to

bed down here. I'll ask a nurse to bring in a cot for Danny. I'll take the chair."

She gazed at the room's one chair. It not only looked uncomfortable, it was also scarcely big enough for Luca's large frame. "You're not going to get much sleep in that."

"I've slept in worse." At her skeptical look, he said, "I'm not leaving you alone." The finality in his voice told her not to argue, but she ignored it.

"I'll be perfectly safe in the hospital. Nobody's going to come after me here."

"Don't be so sure. Drug runners don't play by the same rules as the rest of us. We don't know if someone else is coming after Danny. Or you," he added with emphasis. "It's a fair guess that you are not on the cartel's Christmas list right now."

"The same goes for you."

"They don't know who I am."

"They know you were helping me. That's enough to make them come after you."

"I can take care of myself," he said, voice thick with exhaustion.

"So can I."

He turned away, effectively shutting her out.

Fine.

Sleep was fitful, with nurses and attendants constantly checking on her. At one point, she looked up and saw Luca. Danny had crawled up into his lap and was nestled against his side. Her earlier annoyance forgotten, she smiled at the picture they made. Luca had come through for Danny and her, leaving her with a whole new set of problems.

She'd gone to him for help in rescuing Danny. Somehow, along the way, the past had resurfaced and mixed with the present, awakening feelings within her that she had thought safely stored away.

There could be nothing between her and Luca. They both knew that. There was too much water under the bridge, too many things in the past that couldn't be undone. But there was more.

She'd spent the first two decades of her life under her father's thumb. Since she'd been on her own with Danny, she'd learned to stand up for herself and refused to be bossed by anyone. Luca was a take-charge kind of guy and expected others to do as he said. She wouldn't submit to that. Not again.

So why was she suddenly content to have him close by?

A slight noise outside the door caused Luca to jerk awake. This wasn't any ordinary hospital noise. Hospital sounds had a rhythm to them, the pad of crepe-soled shoes on a linoleum floor, the clang of carts going by. There was a stealthiness to this sound.

On his chest, Danny snored softly, and Luca gave him a gentle shake. "Wake up, Danny. I need you to get in the bathroom and stay there. Don't come out. No matter what." Hadn't he said something like this only last night?

Danny scrambled off his lap and ran to the bathroom.

Luca quickly went to the bed. "Harper. Harper. Someone's here."

She rubbed her eyes, confusion clouding them for only a moment before she nodded.

Luca looked around for a weapon. He'd had to surrender his knife and guns to hospital security, but that didn't mean he was helpless. A container for discarded needles caught his eye, as did a cardboard box for dispensing latex gloves.

He slipped on a pair of gloves, removed the lid from the

container and came away with two needles. He had no idea what they'd been used for, but it didn't matter. A jab from a needle could disorient, maybe even disable an attacker, especially if it was applied at the right spot. Like the eye.

He switched the location of the bed, placing it at an angle. Careful of the IV in Harper's arm, he lifted her and tucked her in the V-shaped space between the bed and adjoining walls.

She didn't waste time asking questions, only nodded her understanding of what he was doing.

He flattened himself behind the door. When it opened, he waited until the man had cleared it and checked his shoes. Not hospital regulation but black wing tips. He grabbed the intruder by his jacket and spun him around, then jabbed him in the neck with the needles.

The man yowled, but he wasn't down. He launched himself at Luca, who planted a fist square in his opponent's face and slammed him into a second man who'd entered behind him. They both went down in a tangle of arms and legs. The second intruder sprang up and pulled a knife from an ankle strap.

The deadly looking weapon sliced through the air and nicked Luca's arm. Ignoring the flash of pain, he sidestepped and narrowly missed being struck again. The limited space didn't give much room to maneuver.

Luca kicked the knife from the assailant's hand and then jabbed his thumbs in the man's eyes. The cry of pain was satisfying, but the battle was only beginning.

The man locked his elbows and lifted them to dislodge Luca's arms. His opponent was massively built and freed himself within seconds. After rubbing his eyes, he sent a look of loathing toward Luca.

Luca didn't react; he was too busy fending off the other guy.

At that moment, an attendant, alerted by the commotion, ran to the room.

"Call security," Luca shouted.

The two tangos looked at each other and then took off.

Luca wanted to follow, but he didn't dare leave Harper and Danny alone. He didn't know if there were others in the hospital who could take up where their compatriots left off.

He lifted Harper from the corner where she'd huddled and settled her on the bed, then opened the door to the bathroom and got Danny.

The little boy was no longer sleepy. His eyes were wide with fear. "Those men wanted to hurt Mommy, didn't they?"

Luca knew he couldn't avoid the question. "Yes, they did. They wanted to hurt all of us."

"But you didn't let them."

"No. I didn't let them." He'd move heaven and earth before he let anyone hurt his son or Harper.

He drew a long breath. The whole thing had seemed to last for a long time, but, in reality, it had been only a few moments from when the men had entered the room until they'd fled. Luca had experienced the phenomena before, the action slowing down to where each movement seemed exaggeratedly slow.

When hospital security showed up, he gave a brief explanation of what had taken place and then called the sheriff's office. The SO promised to relay the message to the sheriff.

Within forty-five minutes, the sheriff showed up. Dressed in typical cowboy garb, from the top of his Stetson to well-worn boots, he looked every inch the Western lawman. To Luca, the man looked like he was trying too hard. His exaggerated drawl only added to the image.

Right away, it became apparent that there was something

between the sheriff and Harper. The tension in the air grew thick. The way he looked at her with an air of possession grated on Luca's nerves.

For her part, Harper smiled at him with friendly warmth but nothing more.

"Caar," she said, "this is Luca Brady. He helped me get Danny back. Luca, Sheriff Caar Davis."

The sheriff stuck out his hand. "Thanks for that, Brady. We're mighty glad to have the boy back."

Luca didn't like how the man referred to Danny as *the boy*.

The sheriff turned his attention to Harper. "You should have come to me," he said, his tone chiding. "We could have handled this."

Her flush revealed her discomfort. "Luca was special forces. I knew he'd know the best way to get Danny back."

Now it was the sheriff who flushed. "Well, I'm glad it worked out, but it's always best to call in the professionals in a case like this. People can get hurt, otherwise," he added with a pointed glance at her wounded shoulder. He shot a what-do-you-have-to-say-for-yourself look at Luca.

Luca didn't react to what was an obvious challenge.

"The important thing is that we got Danny back," Harper said. The sharpness of her tone had the sheriff backing off.

"Of course," he agreed. "Can you tell me what happened? From the very beginning." He took out a small notebook and a pen.

Harper took him through it. At the end of the recitation of facts, Davis put his notebook and pen away. "Doesn't give us much to go on."

"You have Danny's descriptions of the men who took him," Harper said.

"Sure, and we're grateful for that. But a description given

by a five-year-old boy isn't much when it comes to tracking down professionals like these men, what with them wearing masks and all."

A look of consternation flashed in his eyes, but it quickly cleared.

"I'll get this out to my department as well as the state police. One more thing: Vera Dawson was found shot this morning. Her body was left about two miles from town on the old mining road."

Luca put a hand on Harper's shoulder when she gasped.

"Have you told Chuck?" she asked.

"Had to. He took the news as well as can be expected." The sheriff waited a beat. "This was found with her." He produced a note in an evidence bag and gestured for her to read it.

"'This is on you, Harper Sloan.'"

She read it again, silently this time, and her eyes filled with tears.

"You're too smart to believe that," Luca said. He took the note and handed it back to Davis. Luca would have given anything to erase the stricken look from her face.

The sheriff leaned forward and brushed a kiss over Harper's forehead. "I'll be in touch." With that, he started out of the room before turning back to say, "I'll send a deputy out to make sure you get home all right."

Harper sketched a wave in the sheriff's direction. "Thanks."

Luca didn't like the man. He didn't like his dismissal of Danny's description. He didn't like the assumption that he would have handled it better. He especially didn't like the way he'd kissed Harper. None of his business, he told himself. But the honest part of him called himself a liar.

"Something between you and the sheriff?" he asked casually after Davis's departure.

"We've gone out a few times. Nothing serious."

Luca had a feeling that the sheriff saw things differently. "Is that what you think, or does he see it that way, too?"

"Can we drop it?" Her voice turned sharp. "Vera is dead. And it's my fault. If I'd thought things through, maybe—"

He held up a hand. "Stop it. Whoever took Danny and Vera was never going to give them back. At least not alive. You know it, and so do I."

He felt like a heel for focusing on his dislike of the sheriff instead of realizing what the loss of her friend and housekeeper meant to Harper. He remembered Vera from years ago. She'd always treated him decently. "I'm sorry we weren't able to save her."

By the time the deputy showed up, Luca had come up with a plan. There was no way he could leave Harper and Danny on their own at the ranch. He had already planned to take several weeks of vacation from S&J; he'd spend that time beefing up the ranch's security and doing his best to ferret out the drug dealers and put an end to their threats.

He and Harper answered the deputy's questions, which were more in-depth than those of the sheriff. Her frown deepened upon learning about the drug dealers operating in the county. "I thought we'd gotten rid of those varmints around these parts."

Luca smiled at her description of the scum who dealt in drugs, but his lips quickly flattened into a hard line. For every drug dealer taken out, three more sprang up to take his place. There weren't enough prison cells to lock away the men and women who peddled the misery of drug addiction.

Only three days had passed since Harper had shown

up at his home asking for his help, turning his life upside down. His initial anger at her had died, leaving only a profound regret—for the time he had lost with his son. More than anything, he wanted—no, needed—time with Danny, but how would it affect Harper? Hurting her was the last thing he wanted to do.

He pushed that away. For now.

Harper still needed medical care, but he couldn't protect her properly in the hospital. The medical center, which served the entire county, was too vast, and the security too sparse.

The answer was simple: bring an S&J operative, one who had nursing experience, to the ranch to take care of her. A small grin pulled at his lips as he thought of Harper's reaction to hiring a nurse, but he couldn't properly care for her, protect Danny and fortify the ranch security at the same time.

He wasted no time putting his plan into action.

Chuck Dawson met them upon their return to the ranch. The fierce glare he sent in Harper's direction had Luca putting a protective arm around her shoulders.

"You saved your boy but not my Vera," the foreman said. "I should have expected as much."

"Chuck, I'm so sorry about Vera," Harper answered. "If I could have changed things, I would."

Luca drew Harper behind him, wanting to deflect Chuck's anger toward himself. "We were going back for her."

"Too little too late." With that, the foreman stalked off.

Harper's face lost what little color it had had. Despite her protest, Luca lifted her into his arms and carried her upstairs. He left her to change clothes and get into bed while he saw to Danny, helping him clean up.

After Harper was settled in bed, he told her of his plan to bring in an operative/nurse. Her reaction didn't surprise him.

She folded her arms across her chest. "I don't need a nurse."

"Yeah? Who's going to take care of you? Me?"

Her expression told him just what she thought of that.

"You need a trained nurse. It'll only be for a few days," he coaxed. "Once you're back to normal, it's business as usual and you can go back to giving me orders."

When she shifted positions, she winced and nestled her wounded arm to her chest protectively.

"Glad that's settled." It was all he could do to keep the triumph out of his voice. "I've already talked to Ginny Robinson. She'll be here tonight."

"And who is Ginny Robinson?"

"She's a top-flight S&J operative. Plus, she served as a medic in our ranger unit." He paused, waiting for her to absorb everything he'd thrown at her. "You need to be back to full strength to take care of Danny. He's still a target. And so are we since we have the drugs."

Fear flickered in her gaze at the mention of her son. It mixed with indignation. "Pulling out the big guns, Luca?"

"Just trying to keep you and Danny safe. You know this isn't finished." They'd had the conversation before. Now it was time to put it all out there. "The cartel isn't going away. Neither am I." He let that sink in. "I'm not leaving until this is over. So get used to having me around." His gaze challenged hers.

She met it with a fierce one of her own.

Harper had grown into a tough-minded woman. The girl had been strong but untested. This woman had faced her deepest fears when her son had been kidnapped and had come out on top.

What about himself? He feared he didn't measure up to the mantle of strength she wore so easily. He should have stood his ground. Instead, he'd given in to pride and pain when Harper had begged him to leave before the Judge carried through on his threat and put Luca in jail. He could have fought her father's cruelty, but he'd been no match for her tears.

The man had cost Harper and him so many years, years they could have had together. Years where he, Luca, could have watched his son grow and grown deeper in love with Harper.

He thought of what she'd told him about the letters and pictures she'd sent. Back then, he'd had too much pride to go to her and ask why she'd broken her promise to keep in touch with him.

He couldn't blame the Judge for that. No, that was on him.

Now they were back together. What the future held for them, he didn't know.

Events had once pushed Harper and him to their breaking point. He knew they would test their limits again before this was over.

SEVEN

Luca's words tumbling around in her mind, Harper frowned at the gravity of what they were facing. The drug traffickers wanted their merchandise. If they couldn't get it, they'd take it out in revenge. Killing Vera had only been the first step.

Harper hadn't wanted to admit it, but she was grateful that Luca was staying on. Though she prided herself on being able to handle most situations, she knew she wasn't well enough to protect Danny from men who had no reservations about killing a child. For herself, she was willing to take her chances, but not for her son.

Not for Danny.

Never for Danny.

She thought back over the events of the last several days. Something someone had said niggled at the back of her brain, but she couldn't place it. She had a feeling it was important, but the more she tried to identify it, the more elusive it became.

She put it away for now. She had enough on her mind as it was without wondering about something that was obviously not important enough to remember.

Harper was still smarting over the idea that she needed someone to take care of her. She hated the thought of being an invalid.

Ginny Robinson was a pleasant surprise, though, even when she made it clear that she gave the orders. To Harper's amazement, Luca accepted them without protest, and the household ran smoothly under her supervision.

After her initial dislike of the idea of having a nurse, Harper took a liking to Ginny and discovered that they had much in common, including the worries of being a single mother to a young boy.

"My husband was killed five years ago when he deployed overseas. An IED took out the truck he was driving," Ginny said without a trace of self-pity. "Ryan's ten now. He scarcely remembers his father, but I do my best to keep what memories he has alive. He's with my brother right now. Since he has a week off school and my brother can set his own schedule, the two of them went hunting. I'm praying they don't come back with anything. The last thing I want to do is butcher a deer."

The two women shared smiles of understanding.

"Luca told me what's been going on around here. I'm as sorry as I can be about what happened to you and your boy."

"It's not over yet," Harper said with a grimace. "I don't know what I'd have done without Luca."

Ginny gave her an assessing look. "I have a feeling you'd have pulled through. You've got a look about you that says that you'll bend but not break."

Harper considered that one of the nicest compliments she'd ever received. "Thank you."

"You couldn't have a better man than Luca at your side. He and I have been on plenty of operations for S&J together and before that in Afghanistan. He doesn't give up. He just keeps on going until he gets what he's after."

Harper had a feeling the other woman didn't hand out

praise easily, so it said much about Luca to hear that. "You're right."

Ginny didn't let her get away without doing her exercises. Even with the movement, though, Harper grew restless being confined to bed.

She endured Ginny's care for three days. By then, she was tired of being in bed, tired of being waited on, tired of being watched even by someone as easygoing as the good-natured Ginny. When Luca showed up that evening with a tray of soup and fruit, she scowled at him. "Get that out of here and bring me a steak."

"I can see you're feeling better," he said and set the tray on an end table.

"I'll feel even better when I can go on a ride." She usually rode every day except when the cold was too bitter.

He grinned. "Ginny, I don't know how you put up with such a poor patient."

She returned the grin with one of her own. "She's not so bad."

Harper found the grace to smile at the other woman. "Ginny has been great, but even she agrees that I don't need a caretaker any longer."

Ginny nodded. "The patient is ready to be released. Take it easy for a few more days," she instructed Harper. "Remember, you just had a bullet taken out of you."

"Will do. Thank you for everything."

"I'll see you out," Luca said to Ginny, "while the patient eats her soup."

Harper directed another scowl in his direction. She started on the soup, all the while wishing it was a twelve-ounce steak along with a baked potato slathered with butter and sour cream, followed by a big slab of chocolate cake.

When Luca returned, she pushed the tray toward him.

"Now get me some real food." At his raised brow, she added, "Please."

He set the tray back on the nightstand and gave her an assessing look. "You're looking better."

She recognized the tone. He wanted to tell her something and wasn't certain how she'd deal with it.

"Tell me."

"We're not out of the woods as far as the drug traffickers are concerned."

"Like I didn't know that." She flushed at her sarcasm, but she was all out of patience.

"That's why I want to send you and Danny away until this thing is all wrapped up."

"You *want* to send us away?" Her words bristled with resentment. That had been a sore point between them all those years ago, Luca giving orders just as her father had. She hadn't taken them then. She wouldn't be taking them now. Every fiber of her rebelled at the idea.

Then she paused, reconsidering.

It wouldn't be such a bad idea to send Danny away where the bad guys couldn't get to him. The Judge had a younger sister in Salt Lake City. Aunt Luann was always begging Harper and Danny to visit.

"That's not a bad idea. Danny can spend some time with my aunt while you and I deal with the creeps."

"I think you missed the point."

She shook her head. "I didn't miss it at all. I'm not running. This is my fight."

"You're still stubborn as all get out."

"Seems like I heard that before."

"Seems like I said it before."

"You're right. Sending Danny away is probably the best way to keep him safe, but I can't leave. Don't you see? I let the Judge order me around for the first two decades of my life. If I run from this, it'll be like I haven't grown at all. I'll still be that little girl who let herself be bullied by others."

"You really don't know how strong you are, do you?"

She blinked at that. Strong?

"You stood up to the Judge when he wanted you to give Danny away. You raised him all on your own and did a great job of it. You took on drug dealers who were intent on using you and then killing you."

"You did that."

"I was backup. Nothing else. I have no doubt that you could have gotten Danny back on your own if you'd had to."

The air fairly vibrated with tension.

She found her hand mated with his, palms flat, fingers intertwined. How it happened, she didn't know. She didn't remember raising her hand. She didn't remember Luca doing the same. Somehow, though, their hands were now together, the gesture more intimate than she was comfortable with.

Still, she was loathe to remove her hand, loathe to leave the strength and warmth and security his provided. Since when was she looking for strength and warmth and security from a man? She had Danny. He was all she needed.

"I...you..." What was she trying to say? The stuttered words made no sense.

Until Danny, Luca had always occupied first place in her heart. After Luca, there'd never been another man she'd been interested in.

Caar Davis had hinted about something more between them, but that was as far as it had gone. She'd known from the start that there wasn't a future between the sheriff and her. He was good company, and she admired his dedication to his job, but that wasn't enough to build a relationship on. There was something about him that held her back.

"Where do we go from here?" Was she referring to the danger still posed by the drug traffickers or a more personal issue, one between her and Luca? She didn't know.

"We keep you and Danny safe and put an end to the drug trade here."

"That's a pretty big order."

"We need help. I had some ideas about that."

"Would you ask Danny to come in?" she asked. "We need to talk with him about going to Utah."

Danny didn't like the idea of leaving the ranch any more than Harper had. "Are you going, Mommy?"

She shook her head. "No. I have to stay here."

His lip pouted. "If you're staying, then I'm staying, too. I need to take care of you."

Her heart spilled over with love for her child. "We want to keep you safe."

"From the bad guys?" At her nod, he asked, "Will they come find me? There'll only be Aunt Luann to take care of me."

"We'd have you well guarded," Luca said.

"Why can't you do that here?"

Harper sent Luca a helpless look.

"Nothing," he admitted. "That settles it. We're all staying."

Danny nodded in satisfaction. "Good."

"Time for bed," she told him.

The expected protest didn't come, and he clapped a hand over a large yawn.

Luca saw him to bed. "He's a fine boy," he said after returning.

"He's the best thing that ever happened to me."

"You love him a lot."

"With all my heart." Her gaze found his. "Please don't

take him from me. He'll start kindergarten next year. This is the last year he'll have at home." Her voice cracked at the last.

"You think I'd do that?"

"Isn't that what you intend?"

He didn't answer.

Sitting in the living room by himself later, Luca was deep in thought. Not only about the custody issue. Was he making a mistake in giving in on sending Harper and Danny away? Was he allowing his need to have them near jeopardize their safety?

As a ranger commander, he'd made his share of mistakes. He'd also brought his unit through enough harrowing situations to understand that some mistakes can't be made right, no matter how much you might want to.

He was certain that he was where he should be. No one else would fight harder to keep Harper and Danny safe. What he wasn't sure about was what was happening between him and Harper. It wasn't what he expected. Far from it. Whatever they had shared had ended six years ago. Or so he'd thought.

What he felt for her now was not that of the callow boy he'd once been. It was bigger. Deeper. And totally unexpected. Those feelings of years ago paled in comparison to what was in his heart now.

He couldn't lose her again. Nor Danny. Danny had already worked his way into Luca's heart. It wasn't just that he was his son, his own flesh and blood. It was more, so much more, that he was in awe of his own feelings.

That brought him full circle back to why the drug runners had kidnapped Danny. Why not just take Harper and remove the complication of having to take care of a child?

He had tried to wrap his mind around the matter but was no closer to finding answers than he had been.

"Where did you go?" Harper asked when she entered the room. "You looked a thousand miles away."

"I was wondering why the cartel didn't just take you in the first place. Anyone have a grudge against you and want to get back at you through your son?"

"Not that I know of." She harrumphed. "Plenty of people had hard feelings against the Judge, though. He made enemies just by breathing. But me? I haven't lived in the area in years, not since shortly after Danny was born."

"That's what I thought."

She looked thoughtful. "It makes no sense for this to be personal, but you don't agree. You think it's there. Somewhere."

Luca flattened his mouth into a hard line as he nodded. "I keep going over it, but nothing about it makes sense." Logic and reason were the stepping-stones of an ordered life. Who was he kidding? His life hadn't been ordered since Harper had walked back into it.

They had to find out why she and Danny had been targeted. He had a feeling if they could answer that, it would go a long way to answering the other questions that buzzed through his mind. Questions like, why was the cartel only now making such a violent statement in the town? Questions like, were the people in charge planning a big score? Questions like was there somebody on the inside helping them?

An hour later, he was no closer to an answer than he had been before.

Harper looked up from her bookkeeping and drank in the picture father and son made as they read together. Cozied up on the overstuffed leather sofa, Danny nestled at

Luca's side, they read from Danny's favorite book about a family of dinosaurs.

He and Harper had read it so many times that she knew the words from memory, but Danny never tired of hearing the story. Though he had been able to read by himself for a year, he still liked having her read to him. It seemed he felt the same about Luca.

Warmth filled her heart. At the same time, though, she feared what the future would bring.

So many things stood between them, including her fear of heartbreak. Both she and Luca suffered from trust issues stemming from their delicate history. What would she do if she allowed him back into her life and he walked away?

The idea of her son spending half his time in a town sixty miles away caused a lump to form in her throat, but she couldn't rightfully deny Luca having time with his son. It was clear, as well, that Danny was growing to love his father. They were so much alike, not just in looks but in determination.

She knew Danny needed a man in his life, more than what Chuck or the ranch hands could offer.

Before that was settled, though, they had to solve the matter of the drug running. Uneasiness hung over the household like a storm cloud waiting to spew forth its fury. She knew the drug runners weren't finished with her family. They'd come at them again, attacking when least expected.

Vera's funeral had been held that morning. With Chuck's permission, they'd buried her in the family graveyard. The foreman had apologized for his accusations and thanked Harper for making the arrangements.

"I don't know what came over me," he said, "going after you that way. Wasn't your fault any more than it was mine."

The service had been attended by the ranch hands and a

few townspeople. Vera had kept to herself, more so after her arthritis had turned bad. For Chuck's sake, Harper wished more people had turned out, but at least Vera had been remembered.

More than anything, she longed for this all to be over. She was depending on Luca to keep them safe. When was the last time she'd depended upon anyone other than herself?

As though aware that he was the subject of her thoughts, he lifted his gaze and looked at her, his eyes full of questions. She averted her gaze, unable to answer what she read in his.

She felt like a boat pilot navigating new and uncharted waters. She was hesitant to read too much into the changed feelings between her and Luca. After they'd cleared up the mix-up of the letters, much of Luca's anger about not knowing about Danny had dissolved.

Despite that, their relationship was still fraught with uncertainty and a new kind of tension all its own. While she was grateful for the warmer feelings between them, she didn't know what to expect for the future.

A taut silence stretched between them, but the tension seemed to be bleeding away, and a new sort of sensation now filled the space, one she shied away from attempting to identify.

A shiver caused her to wrap her upper arms around herself to keep warm. She did her best to convince herself that it was due solely to the danger the drug runners still presented, but she knew better. It was Luca's nearness that sent goosebumps tracking their way down her spine.

There had been no talk of the future, much less a future together. Still, she couldn't help but dream that she, Luca and Danny could be a family.

But that was all it was. A dream.

EIGHT

Changes.

She could hear them, feel them. It was in the sough of the wind, the low of the cattle, the snap of cold in the air.

The morning's vibrant blue sky intensified the cold. Though it seemed contradictory, a clear sky made for colder temperatures since there was no cloud cover. It was only part of what made living in Colorado a study in ambiguities.

The changes in her were more subtle but just as strong. The feelings she'd had for Luca six years ago had changed. They were those of a woman now. How had she ever let him go? Shame washed through her as she recalled in painful detail how weak and foolish she'd been in allowing her father to bully her into walking away from her marriage. He'd done it, of course, under the pretext of helping her.

It had taken only a few months to discover that he'd done it for himself. By that time, she'd learned she was expecting a child. Her refusal to "give up the brat" as her father had put it had cemented her decision to leave the ranch. She hadn't stepped foot on it again until she'd learned of his final illness.

She wandered to the tall windows that flanked the fireplace, pulled aside the heavy curtains and gazed outside.

The land. Always the land. She loved it. It held its own

kind of beauty. At the same time, it gave no quarter to those who didn't respect it.

It drew her, the sheer vastness of it. Despite the dangers it held, the harsh and often unforgiving nature of it, the magnificence of the Lord's handiwork never failed to fill her with awe. The Lord had created it, and she and others were called to be not owners, but stewards over it. How could she not be moved by it?

A favorite scripture, Psalm 24:1–2, came to mind: "The earth is the Lord's, and the fulness thereof; the world, and they that dwell therein. For he hath founded it upon the seas, and established it upon the floods."

She turned her attention back to Luca and Danny. Father and son, dark heads bent together, almost touching. Once again, she was grateful Luca was here. He had beefed up security in every part of the ranch, from reinforcing the gates and fences to installing alarms at every entrance, including the barn and outbuildings. No one came or went without it registering.

She didn't like the feeling of living in locked-down conditions, but she understood the need.

Still, she was grateful when Luca reminded her it was time for their morning ride.

It had become a habit for Harper and Luca to ride fence in the morning. After much discussion, they had arranged for two of the most experienced ranch hands to watch over Danny. Luca had made sure that both men were armed and knew how to handle themselves. There was no way that they would leave their son unprotected.

Overseeing the security measures was a part of it, yes, but there was more. The rides, away from the business of running the ranch and keeping an eye on Danny, gave them time to bridge the six-year gap that separated them. They were getting to know each other all over again.

Once they mounted their horses and set out, their gazes met, and a sweet warmth surged through her. Though it lasted only a few seconds, it was the nicest interruption she'd had during these last harrowing days, a bright moment in what had been a terrifying week.

Today, she was taking him to the north ridge. It was a long ride, but it offered an unparalleled view of the valley where the ranch house was nestled.

In the summer, fields stretched into the horizon, a green-and-brown quilt stitched with streams and roads. The colors traded places every year as farmers plowed under the previous year's crops and let the fields lay fallow while other sections were planted for the new season.

She had plans for the land. Big plans. She wanted to convert part of it to organic farming and ranching. Demand for organic products was growing with every year. One time, she had tried talking with her father about introducing new methods into their operation. She'd come prepared with facts and figures, even a spreadsheet showing how long it would take to recoup the initial investment of converting traditional methods to organic.

He'd shut her down immediately.

She'd never approached him again. About anything.

The view, beautiful as it was, was not one of peace. Not today. Fresh snow blanketed the ground, but it wasn't a "winter wonderland" scene. Instead, it was one of hardship and backbreaking work. Getting up at five in the morning to take feed to the cattle, separating the weaker from those able to withstand the cold, repairing fences that had snapped under their heavy blankets of snow—all were part of a rancher's lot in a Colorado winter. And then there was the breaking up of ice that had formed on top of the watering troughs. Contrary to what many thought, cattle couldn't eat snow.

She loved this land, but she wasn't immune to the price it exacted upon those who chose to make their home there. The city contained a myriad of attractions, but it had never held her heart as did the land that would always be home.

"Penny for your thoughts," Luca said as he pulled his horse beside hers.

Her thoughts? How did she convey the pull she felt for this piece of earth? Some saw it as barren, but others, like her, saw the beauty. What did Luca see when he looked at it? What did he feel?

"Would you ever think of settling somewhere like this?" She clamped her lips together. Why had she asked that? It was practically an admission of her hopes for a future with him.

"I don't know. Depends on who I'd be sharing it with."

His answer stirred a measure of hope in her. Could he be contemplating a future with her as well? She didn't have the courage to broach that subject.

Most of their conversations had focused on Danny and the trauma he'd experienced. Should they have him see a therapist? Or should they let him take the lead and be guided by that? Seeing a professional could help with the night terrors he was experiencing. On the other hand, she didn't want him to think that something was wrong with him.

She had voiced her concerns aloud, wanting Luca's input. He needed to be part of this. A wry smile curved her lips at the thought of his reaction if she were to try to keep him out of it.

Already, he and Danny had bonded. When she saw them

together, she was taken aback by how much the son resembled the father. The same dark hair that refused to stay in place after it was combed. The same steady gaze. Even their walk was the same, Danny's stride a miniature of Luca's much longer one.

She had come to terms with sharing custody of Danny with Luca if it came to that. At the same time, she knew that heartache was inevitable for those times when Danny lived with his father.

There were no easy answers. Since their last talk, they had shied away from the subject, knowing that to bring it to light would upset the fragile balance they'd managed to achieve. Just the thought of it had her heartbeat racing and her throat getting raspy, as though she had a cold. Maybe that was it. A cold.

But she knew she was lying to herself.

Aware of the silence that stretched between them now, she turned in her saddle and started to say something when a Jeep showed up, traveling faster than the snow warranted.

They met the driver.

"Caar," she said, "what's up?"

Sheriff Davis climbed out of the vehicle and pulled his hat farther down over his head. "Me and my boys checked out the campsite where Danny was being held. Not a sign. Everything you described is gone."

"We expected as much," Luca said.

"We'll keep looking."

Harper smiled at the sheriff. "We appreciate you keeping us in the loop."

"No problem." With a tip of his hat, he was gone.

"Awful long way to come to tell us that he didn't have anything," Luca observed.

"I suppose he's doing the best he can." She lifted her

gaze to the darkening sky. "Looks like another storm is brewing. Let's head for home."

As one, they turned the horses toward the ranch house and made the ride in near silence. When the shot came, Luca grabbed her from her saddle and swung her to the ground, protecting her body with his own. The horses took off.

Two more shots peppered the ground.

"Luca?" she asked.

"I'm okay. You?"

"Same." Her teeth chattered, but not from cold. From stark fear. "Who is it?" Stupid question. The cartel members had a grudge to settle, but coming this close to the ranch was asking for trouble, with Luca having armed all the men. How had they managed to bypass all the new security measures?

"Stay low," he said. "We have to make it to those boulders." An outcropping of boulders jutted up from the snow. As it was, they were out in the open, an easy target for the shooter.

They zigzagged across the ground and managed to dodge the bullets.

When they reached the boulders and scrambled into a crevice, Harper drew a long breath. When the horses returned to the ranch without them, Chuck would send a search party. For now, though, they were on their own.

"How many do you figure there are?" she asked.

"At least two."

Both she and Luca were armed. They could fend off two shooters, but if more showed up, they were in trouble.

"How did they get on the ranch without being spotted? Without us getting an alert?" Luca's safety measures not only detected intruders but would also send an alarm to both of them. "It's not possible."

"Unless they had help."

She frowned over that. There was no one on the inside who would hurt her or Danny. Of that, she was positive. She knew Luca had made certain that they had the best security measures available and had hired S&J's technical team to make it happen. He'd also picked out the gates and had personally overseen their installation as well as the reinforcement of padlocks on all the outbuildings. Ranch hands were now armed with instructions to "shoot first and ask questions later."

Still, she felt bound to protest any hint that one of her people was disloyal, but a look at the hard set to Luca's eyes kept her silent. For now, they had to get out of here. There'd be time enough later to find out how the breach had happened.

Luca assessed the situation. The boulders provided scant protection from the gunshots sent their way, but there was no other cover. His rifle was strapped to his horse, now long gone. His Glock was a powerful weapon, but it was no match for the long-range rifles they were facing.

"We need something to lure the shooters out in the open," he said.

"I've got an idea. I'll pretend to make a run for it. When they start shooting, I'll hit the ground, play like I'm hit."

"And if you're really hit?"

"You said we needed something to draw them out. After a few minutes, you run toward me and make like you're going to bring me back to the boulders. When they shoot, you pretend that you're hit. That way, the shooters will think they've succeeded. When they come to check it out, we take them out."

Before he could point out all the things that could go wrong with the plan, Harper got in a running crouch and took off. The expected shots rang out, and she fell. Either she was really good at playacting, or she'd been hit.

She remained still for long minutes. Keeping low, Luca ran to her, afraid of what he would find. Her wink reassured him. He feigned checking her pulse. Another shot, and he dropped to the ground.

It wasn't long before he heard footsteps. *Don't rush it. Keep playing dead.* Heavy breathing told him that someone was now standing directly over him.

He grabbed the weapon and pulled it from the man's hand.

Startled, the attacker didn't resist until it was too late.

A crack of sound later, the man fell, a neatly placed bullet wound centered in his forehead.

Keeping the assailant's body as a barrier between him and the second shooter, Luca aimed the rifle, trying to pinpoint where the shot came from. When he had a bead on the man, he fired. A sharp cry confirmed he had nailed the shooter.

Luca kept his hand on Harper's back, urging her to stay down. Though he didn't think there were any more shooters, he couldn't be certain. When he decided enough time had passed, he stood and helped her up.

She brushed the snow from her. "Why shoot his partner and not us?" she asked.

"My guess is that he didn't want to take any chances on us getting the partner back to town and questioning him." Seeing that she was trembling, Luca wrapped his arms around her, gratified when she nestled to him and buried her head against his shoulder. "The important thing is that we're okay. Right?"

"Right." But she didn't sound certain.

He understood. Seeing a man shot down in front of you wasn't an experience you soon forgot, even if he had been intent on killing you.

He took her hand. "C'mon. Let's get out of here."

The trek back to the ranch house was made in near silence. Part of it stemmed from the energy they had to expend in tramping through the deep snow, which made talking difficult, but part, he knew, was from shock.

When he saw Harper's lips moving, he knew that she was praying. He had turned his back on the Lord since his deployment to Afghanistan, the Stand, where he'd witnessed so many atrocities that his heart had shut down. Could he summon the belief in God that had once been such an important part of his life? Maybe it was time he tried.

Before he could make the attempt, two riders showed up.

When Chuck and another ranch hand showed up with the horses, Harper gave a cry of relief. Her legs burned with the effort of navigating the knee-high snow. She rushed to the small search party and hugged Hank, threading her hands in his lush mane.

After Chuck dismounted, she hugged him as well. "Thank you. I knew you'd come."

"Sorry it took so long. I was tending a sick mare and didn't learn that your horses had returned without you until a short while ago."

"You came. That's all that matters."

Luca and Chuck exchanged stiff nods. The two men had never warmed up to each other. She hoped that would change as they got to know each other better.

They made short work of the trip back to the ranch house. There, they went in search of Danny and found him in the barn with Tommy Shawcroft, a new ranch hand.

"Look, Mommy." He pointed to the clean hay in three stalls. "Tommy's letting me help."

"I hope that's all right," Tommy said with a deferential smile at Harper.

"It's just fine. Thanks for watching over him."

Tommy brushed a hand over Danny's head. "Danny and me are pals. Right?"

"Right."

Danny slipped his hand inside Luca's much larger one. Harper drew a sharp breath at how right they looked together.

"I need to clean up. Can Danny stay with you?" she asked.

Luca looked as though he'd just won a prize. "Sure thing."

Secure in the knowledge that Danny was safe with Luca, Harper returned to the house. A layer of snow mixed with dirt covered her clothes, and she needed to shower. Plus, the picture of the dead man, lying only a foot from where she'd been, made her want to scrub away the image.

But how did she scrub away death itself?

NINE

With Danny down for a nap and Harper asleep after her shower, Luca had met with the sheriff and two deputies, first reporting the shooting incident and then showing them where the body was.

When he'd returned from that unpleasant duty, he had double-checked the security measures he'd installed, looking for any holes. Things were buttoned up as tightly as he remembered, so how had the two shooters penetrated the security?

He couldn't get past the idea that someone from the inside had helped them. He pushed it from his mind for now; he had ranch work to see to. After bundling up once more, he headed to the barn, a smile on his mouth. He'd discovered that he liked what he called barn chores. The steady rhythm of cleaning the stalls, scooping out old hay and replacing it with new, gave his muscles a good workout. Both evened out the ragged crop of questions the last few days had sown.

Needing the routine, he started on the tack, rubbing oil into the supple leather. Unable to escape his thoughts, Luca pulled up the conversation with the sheriff and replayed it in his mind. Unlike Harper, who believed the sheriff was doing the best he could, Luca wasn't so sure. If he had returned with that paltry bit of information to his unit commander, he'd have had his butt chewed out but good.

He'd noted that the sheriff carried a Glock, much like his own. The Glock was a serviceable weapon with a short recoil. The polymer framed semiautomatic was featured regularly in television and movies. For that reason, as well as its light weight, it was a popular weapon. But it was the AK-47 strapped to the back of the Jeep that had really caught Luca's interest, and he wondered when the sheriff had an opportunity to use it. He didn't look like the kind of man who carried a weapon only for show.

Had it only been a coincidence that he had been in the area shortly before the shooting started? Could he have been the second shooter?

Luca closed his eyes and tried to pull something up, something the sheriff had said. It nagged at him, but he couldn't place it. He had a feeling it could be important, but the more he tried to identify it, the more elusive it became.

Once again, he went through the brief words they'd exchanged. Nothing there to set off an alarm. He'd met the sheriff one other time. Was there something there that today's dialogue set off?

He put it away. He had other things to think about, things like what he would do once this was over, things like how he and Harper would share custody of their son. The idea was at once exhilarating, and at the same time, left a sour taste in his mouth. Could he really take Danny away from Harper even part time?

Despite his resolve to keep his relationship with her focused solely on protecting her and Danny, his feelings for her had deepened over the short amount of time since she'd come back into his life. He was playing with fire, and he knew it.

He hadn't thought he could forgive her for keeping his son from him, but he had. Even before they'd figured out her father's treachery, he had known he couldn't hold a grudge against her. He hadn't wanted to be attracted to her again, but he was. He hadn't wanted to have feelings for her.

But he did.

Not only was he risking his heart, he was also risking Danny's life. He couldn't allow himself to be distracted by his feelings for Harper. The men who took him could show up at the ranch anytime, wanting retribution and their drugs. His concentration had to be here, on his son. *His son.* The words never failed to thrill him.

He kept at his self-imposed task until the tack was as supple as suede. The comparison only served to remind him of how Harper had looked in the suede pants and shirt she'd worn earlier today.

Enough.

"You about finished?" Chuck asked, coming up beside him.

"Yeah."

The foreman took a look at the tack. "Missed a spot," he said, pointing to a slightly darker area.

Luca hadn't missed anything. The spot was simply a natural shading in the fine leather, but he nodded and went back over it. Chuck had yet to warm up to him. Luca chalked it up to his protectiveness of Harper and Danny but couldn't help wondering if there was something he'd done that had caused the foreman's dislike.

"What put a burr up your butt?" he asked.

Chuck Dawson lifted a shoulder in a negligent shrug. "Don't know what you're talking about."

"Don't you? You've had a grudge against me ever since I

showed up. I'm trying to keep Danny and Harper safe, but you've done your best to block everything I've tried to do."

The foreman gave him a scowl that would scour paint from a barn door. "You got no right talking to me that way. I've been with Harper a lot of years. She knows who she can count on. And who she can't." Dawson speared him with a look that said he had more to say, something that would hurt Luca as nothing else would. "I'm not the one who walked out on her six years ago."

In his years as a ranger and then as an operative for S&J, he had been trained to look for what didn't fit. He hadn't imagined the foreman's coldness toward him. He didn't re-call Dawson being cold to him six years ago, but he hadn't really paid much attention to anyone but Harper back then.

The answer came with such a dawning awareness that he chastised himself that he hadn't thought of it earlier. Luca had saved Danny, but he hadn't saved Dawson's wife, Vera. No wonder the man had no use for him.

"About Vera—"

"Don't use her name. Not ever. You're not fit to say it."

Luca couldn't fault the foreman for his anger. The best thing to do was to keep his distance. He finished cleaning his tools, stored them away, then headed to the house. Still, he couldn't help wondering if there was more at play here.

Luca paced the length of the library/office and back again. He had repeated the path so many times that Harper was certain the hardwood floor now bore the imprint of his shoes.

She shared his restlessness.

She knew he was chafing at the waiting game the enemy was playing. Waiting for the drug runners' next attack.

Waiting for information that could help the authorities break the back of the whole operation. Waiting.

She was grateful that Luca had already handed over the drugs to the DEA. She hadn't wanted them in her home any longer than necessary.

"This is the hardest part," he said, apparently reading her mind. "Waiting for the enemy to make their move."

"You must have done a lot of that when you were with the rangers."

"Too much. I remember one time when our unit was on standby, waiting for intel from our people to go in and take out a group of insurgents who were holding a whole village hostage. It got bad enough that one of our guys said he was going in no matter what command said. Going in without authorization could get him court-martialed and even thrown in prison. We got him calmed down, but he was only saying what the rest of us felt."

She had a bad feeling about what he was going to say next. "What happened?" Part of her didn't want to hear it; part of her knew she had to if she was going to understand this man.

Luca pressed the pads of his thumbs into the corners of his eyes. "When we finally got the word that we could move, we walked into a scene that had many of the men falling to their knees and sobbing."

"Lots of fighting?"

"Just the opposite. The insurgents had pulled up stakes and left, but not before they had murdered every man, woman and child they could find. Some of the people hid in the mountains, but a lot more were slaughtered.

"The village looked like a war zone. The bodies…" His voice broke off. She didn't try to hurry him, understanding he was searching for words to describe the unspeakable.

When he started again, she almost reached for his hand, stopped herself. The pain in his eyes told her this was a journey for which he did not want company. "The only thing left for us to do was to bury the dead. Before we could get started, the villagers who had survived came trickling back. What got me most was the quiet. There was no crying, no weeping. Only the sounds of a people doing the only thing they knew how to do: bury their dead and get on with the business of living."

"How did you go on?" Luca would have internalized what happened. Of that, she was certain.

"Like the villagers, we didn't have a choice." He shook his head. "They had seen horrors that we can't even picture, but they refused to give up. My men and I returned to our headquarters, filed a report and tried to forget what we'd seen. The only problem was that those images never went away. They were burned into our minds as if we'd been branded with them."

She wanted to close her eyes to the scene he had described, but that wouldn't blank out the cruelty and devastation.

"And after that?"

"You mean after I stopped blaming myself?"

She wasn't surprised that he'd blamed himself.

"You couldn't have stopped it."

"If I had pushed harder for permission to take out those insurgents, we might have saved a whole lot of lives. Instead, I sat there, knowing what was happening and that I couldn't do anything about it."

She wanted to comfort him, to take the weight of his pain away. And knew she couldn't. Only the Lord could do that, and, as Luca had told her, he wasn't exactly on speaking terms with Him.

"I resigned my commission after that. I couldn't keep doing what I'd been doing. I came back to the States, bummed around for a bit before I signed on with S&J. It saved my life."

What did she say? *I'm sorry* was a paltry offering. It wasn't enough, not nearly enough. In the end, she settled for reaching for his hand and simply holding it. The hand was like the man himself: big, hard, strong. But she knew he would never use his strength against the innocents of the world. No. He would defend those who could not do so for themselves.

"You suffered over this." She saw the pain in his eyes and knew that he was still suffering.

A perplexed expression crossed his face. "I've never told anyone outside of the brass what happened. I'm sorry. You didn't need to hear that."

But she did.

Before she could say anything, he headed for the door, his stride long and angry.

"Luca?"

He turned, paused, his expression stony and set.

She didn't know at whom his anger was directed. Her? Or himself? "Please, don't go."

The expression in his eyes was guarded, as though he wasn't certain of his next move.

"I shouldn't have told you that."

"Why not?"

"Because..."

"Because why?"

His shrug said he didn't know. She held out a hand. "Stay. Please."

Luca wondered why he'd shared that story with Harper. He had wished for another time and place, but neither would have changed the horror of the story. Not even his buddies at S&J knew the full details of the incident. Merely thinking about it normally caused spasms of misery to course through him. Strangely, though, telling her of that day eased some of the remembered pain. How was that possible?

It didn't make sense, yet there it was.

"Your heart is still hurting," she said. She didn't make it a question, and he didn't take it as such.

He gave a short nod and then a shrug, as if to shake off the memories and the conversation. He wasted no time switching subjects. "I want to talk with your foreman."

"I told you everything Chuck told me."

"I still want to talk with him."

"Afraid that I missed something?"

"Maybe he'll remember something that he forgot to tell you."

She nodded. "Go easy on him, okay? He just lost his wife." She punched in a number on her phone. "Chuck, can you meet us in the office?"

The ranch office was the hub of the operation. The Judge had spent most of his time there when he wasn't in the city. Since Harper had returned to the ranch, she'd taken it over because its rightful owner, her son, was too young. The memories it held weren't pleasant, but she'd decided she couldn't allow the past to rule her any longer.

When Chuck showed up, he and Luca gazed at each other warily. The two men, separated by a generation, had much in common. Both tall and lanky. Both with skin weathered by the elements. Both given to few words, but what words they said tended to count.

"Harper's taken me through what you told her about the kidnapping incident, but I'd like to hear it again," Luca said.

Chuck recounted the story as he'd told it to her.

"Was there anything about the men that seemed familiar?" Luca asked. "I get that they were wearing masks, but maybe the way they moved, the way they talked. Anything at all?"

"Nothing that stands out," the foreman said. "I wish there was. Twenty years ago, they'd have had a fight on their hands. I wouldn't have rolled over like I did."

"It wasn't your fault, Chuck," Harper said. "You couldn't have prevented what happened."

"I'd have sure tried."

She patted his shoulder. "I know."

He turned to Luca. "Anything else?"

"No. Thanks."

Chuck walked out.

Luca did a quick mental review of what he'd learned from the foreman. Unfortunately, it wasn't much, just as it had been with the sheriff.

"When did you start doing search-and-rescue?" Luca asked.

Harper was relieved to talk about something other than the kidnapping and drugs.

"Shortly after I returned here. I'd always been active in helping to find people lost in the mountains. The ranch is expensive to run, and I needed a way to pay the bills. This work fits."

"You always were a natural when it came to the outdoors."

Aside from earning her a living, finding people gave her a purpose. Her reputation had grown. She didn't regret the decision. Until now. Now she rued the day she had ever volunteered for the first rescue mission.

"You have to know this isn't your fault," Luca said.

Had he read her mind? He'd always known her better than she had known herself. It seemed that hadn't changed.

Luca's countenance grew grim. "Does Danny understand that we're not out of danger? I don't want him alone for a minute. Not outside."

"How far do you think the cartel will take this? They have to know that we'll be ready if they come at us again."

"I don't put anything past scum like that." He rubbed his thumb over his chin, a gesture Harper recognized to mean he was working something through in his mind.

She didn't ask questions and allowed him the quiet he needed.

"Did you ever think that this could be an inside job?" he asked after long minutes of silence.

"No." The answer came automatically.

She trusted her men. After the Judge's death, many of the ranch hands had quit. She hadn't tried to persuade them to stay. She'd advertised online and through word of mouth that she was looking for men who weren't afraid of hard work in return for superior pay. She had carefully vetted the men who'd shown up. Each one had proven himself.

"There's no one who has a beef with you? No one who thinks he's being underpaid? No one who was let go or that you called out for some reason?"

She shook her head. "I pay the highest wages in the area. My men are loyal."

"And Chuck?"

"Chuck's been with the ranch longer than I've been alive. He and Vera—" she gulped "—practically raised me. I have no reason to doubt him." Her voice rose at the last.

"Don't go getting your feathers ruffled."

"My feathers are just fine, thank you."

"Are you sure? From where I'm standing, they're looking a little ragged." He stuffed his hands inside his pockets, giving her the impression of an old West cowboy.

"Maybe you should see to your own feathers."

They stared at each other, and she realized that she didn't want to argue with him. She wanted to go back to the easy footing they'd established. She didn't know what the future held for her and Luca, but she very much wanted to find out.

"Sorry," she said. "I know you're just looking out for Danny and me."

Luca gave a short nod, telling her that he'd drop the subject for now, but he wasn't finished with this.

Luca didn't like what he was thinking. Thoughts of what could have happened to Danny if they hadn't gotten him back tormented his mind, bringing up images that terrified him far more than any memories of what he'd endured overseas.

No one would get to Danny or Harper, he vowed. Not on his watch. Which brought him to another problem.

He couldn't return to S&J. Not as long as his son and ex-wife were in danger.

They needed him. Almost as much as he needed them.

Next came a call to Gideon, explaining that he wouldn't be returning to work anytime soon.

"I'm okay," he said. "But I'm needed here for a while longer. Until these lowlifes are locked up and put away, I'm not leaving my family alone." *My family.* Where had those words come from? Had he come to think of Harper and Danny as family? A dangerous thought, he told himself.

There was no hesitation on Gideon's part. "Stay as long as you need," he said. "Family comes first. Always."

Gideon and his wife had two little girls, both pistols, and were expecting a third child in the spring.

Luca had always dismissed the idea of having a family, believing it impossible. Now, he wondered. Was it possible that he could be part of a family? With the rangers, he'd been trained as an apex predator to take out the enemy as quickly and efficiently as possible. Could he set that part of himself aside when he was home and become the husband and father he'd always hoped he could be?

Could he have a real family with Harper and Danny? He and Harper still had to work through the quagmire of the past, and he had no illusions that it would be easy. They had to learn to adjust to each other's demanding personality. Would that even be possible? Dare he hold on to a thread of hope that they could do it?

Abruptly aware that Gideon was still on the line, Luca said, "Thanks. I'll keep in touch."

The dream of a family, with a house full of children, a big sloppy dog and bikes littering the driveway, was just that. A dream. But, oh, how he wished it was more.

He reminded himself that he was here to do a job. If he wanted to protect Danny and his mother, he'd better get to work. Standing around idle wasn't his style.

Neither was wishing for what could never be.

TEN

Harper retreated to the library, where she worked on the books. With the money she made from her search-and-rescue business, plus selling part of the cattle, the ranch would remain solvent for another month, two, if she stretched things out.

She then turned her attention to developing online ads and updating her website. Other S-and-R outfits had sprung up in the area, and she had to keep up or be left behind.

Money had been tight on the ranch when she was younger. When she'd returned, though, she'd noticed freshly painted outbuildings and new equipment, including a generator for those times when the power went out.

She wanted to start employing more modern techniques for ranching to target the organic market. But change took time. Time and money.

Chuck burst into the library. "Harper. There's something wrong with Hank. We can't get him up."

Harper pushed back her chair and stood. Paperwork could wait. The reasons behind a horse not being able to get up varied. And none of them were good. After grabbing her coat, hat and gloves, she followed Chuck to the barn and strode toward Hank's stall. She found the big gelding in his stall, contentedly munching on hay. "What're you talking about? Hank looks fine."

"He is," Chuck said. "It was just the best way I knew to get you here without you asking a lot of questions."

"I'm here. What's so important?" She worked to keep the impatience from her voice. She had a mountain of paperwork to attend to. More importantly, she wanted to spend time with Danny.

"We got us some settling up to do." Chuck didn't sound like himself. His voice was hoarse, like he was getting a cold. But there was something else as well. Something in his eyes, dark and menacing.

"What kind of settling up?"

He grabbed her arm and yanked her toward him. "Don't make a sound. You and me are going on a little field trip."

She tried to wrench away, but his grip on her arm tightened, causing her to wince. "I don't understand." She wasn't frightened, only confused. This was Chuck, a friend her whole life. He would never hurt her.

Was he having some kind of breakdown over Vera's death? She'd done her best to support him, to be a listening ear if he needed one.

He bound her hands with a short length of rope then marched her toward the rear of the barn to a parked Jeep. Normally, vehicles weren't parked there but kept in the oversized garage designed to hold all the ranch transportation. Roughly, he pushed her inside.

"Of course, you don't," he said, answering her question. "You're too busy being Harper Sloan, daughter of Judge Calvin Sloan, shooting star of the county. The whole state. And now you're some kind of big shot search-and-rescue star. Why should you understand anything about me?"

The angry words and nasty tone weren't like him. For the

first time, a frisson of real fear shimmied down her spine. Impatiently, she tamped it down. Chuck had been at her side when her first horse, a sweet mare named Gemma, died of colic. He'd held her while she cried out her heart because the Judge had been too busy to be there.

"What have I done to make you so angry?" She hoped her voice was calmer than was the churning in her stomach.

"You really don't know, do you?"

"No. I don't."

He pushed her down. "Stay down."

"Chuck, you're scaring me."

"Good."

They rode for a short distance before he told her she could get up.

Well and truly frightened now, she asked, "Why? Why are you doing this?"

The irony of asking the same question she'd voiced upon learning of Danny's kidnapping wasn't lost on her.

"You want to know why? Best you ask your pa." He chuckled at the joke. "He'd tell you why. Then again, maybe he wouldn't. He never did like admitting he was in the wrong."

"What did he do?"

"You know as well as I do."

"No, I don't." When Chuck sent her a disbelieving look, she said, "I promise. I don't." She stared at the man she'd thought was a friend. "It was you?" The bile of betrayal burned her throat, and she tried to swallow it back.

"Yeah. It was me. Who do you think set it up to snatch the kid in the first place? At first, it was going to be you, but I knew taking Danny would make you work that much harder to get the drugs."

Harper worked to wrap her mind around the fact that

the man she'd thought of as an uncle, a friend, had done this. Put her son in jeopardy. Her, too.

"Why?"

His answer came swiftly. "The money was too good to say no to. I owed a bunch of money to an online gaming site. Thanks to Cal, I didn't have many options."

What did her father have to do with it? "What happened between you and the Judge?"

"Don't pretend that you don't know."

Bewildered, she shook her head. "I don't know. Why don't you tell me?"

Chuck huffed. "Your old man was so cheap he'd steal the bark off a dog if he could've found a way to do it."

That tracked. The Judge had been notorious for his miserly ways.

"But he always promised me that the ranch would be mine once he passed," Chuck continued. "Then he learned that he was dying and changed his will to give everything to your boy. Just like that. I was out."

"That's not on Danny. Or me. That's on the Judge."

"I took what was mine. And I'd do it again."

"Turns out you're just like my father after all. Greedy and mean-spirited. All you care about is yourself."

"That ain't fair. I stood by your old man for more than twenty-five years, seeing to his every need, and what did he leave me but a measly ten thousand dollars. The ranch should have been mine. It should have all been mine."

Venom dripped from every word. So, this was what it was all about. Vengeance toward the Judge. It seemed that the old man could still hurt her after all.

"Danny didn't do anything to you. He didn't ask that the ranch be left to him."

"You're right. That boy of yours didn't do nothing, nothing to deserve the ranch. He didn't sweat alongside Cal for years, working to make the land worth something. While Cal was off being judge, who do you think took over the work? I sweated blood building this place up. Your pa hardly had a kind word for me, but I kept at it, thinking it would be mine someday."

"Why didn't you tell me?"

"Would you have believed me?"

"Yes." She could see the Judge making a promise and then reneging on it. Though he had preached honesty and morality, he'd never held himself to the same standards.

"I didn't see you offering me any part of it. You kept me on, but you saw me as a hired hand, just like your pa did. I worked my butt off for him, smoothed things over when he got in a ruckus with the other ranchers, took care of him when he turned sickly."

"Why didn't you say anything?" she asked again. "If it was the ranch you wanted, I would have gladly given it to you to keep my son safe. You could have come to me, told me what the Judge promised. I would have worked with you."

"I don't go begging to anyone." He gave her a baleful look. "Don't try to pretend that you didn't want the ranch. You saw dollar signs when you learned that Cal gave it to the boy."

She ignored that. "And Vera? Was she in on it, too?"

He barked out a laugh. "Vera? Nah. Though she wouldn't have said no to the money. She was forever after me to ask the Judge for a raise. It got to where I couldn't stand the sound of her voice, nagging, always nagging. One of my conditions in setting up the kidnapping was that they take her, too." He waited a beat. "And then get rid of her."

She tried to wrap her brain around what he'd said. "You wanted her dead?"

"Why not? When she wasn't nagging me, she was complaining about how much she hurt. A man can only stand so much."

Horror at what he'd done numbed her mind, and she looked at him in revulsion. "You're a monster."

It was as if she was seeing Chuck for the very first time. The real Chuck.

"What do you plan on doing now?" she asked in a shockingly calm voice.

"I'm going to turn you over to the cartel. I searched the ranch, couldn't find hide nor hair of them drugs. That boyfriend of yours will turn them over right quick once he learns they have you."

But Luca no longer had the drugs. Chuck and his conspirator friends didn't know that, but once they did, Harper knew she was as good as dead.

She knew that Luca would move heaven and earth to get her back, but he couldn't fight the whole gang of drug runners.

"If it's money you want…" she started.

"Money's fine, but I want the ranch."

"What are you going to do?"

"I told you. I'm turning you over to Delgado and his friends. They'll pay plenty for you."

Delgado. Where had she heard that name before? It came back on a rush of fear as she recalled hearing it at the drug runners' camp. Delgado was the name of the boss. El Jefe.

"Don't do this. Please." She hated being reduced to begging.

A whiff of regret crossed his face before his mouth set in a hard line. "It's been done." The finality in his voice told her that she had no hope of convincing him to change his mind.

Harper understood that Chuck would never let her go. Greed and revenge made a nasty mix.

He cast a quick, dark glance her way. "Don't be thinking about trying something. Delgado and his men don't care if you're roughed up. In fact, they'd prefer it."

"You'd do that?"

"I've waited a long time for what's mine. If I have to rough you up a bit, it's no skin off me."

"I never really knew you at all, did I?" How had she been so blind? All these years, she'd thought Chuck was a friend. He'd even protected her from the Judge's wrath at times.

"You saw what you wanted to see. Your father's gofer. Now you're seeing the man who's going to take what's his." The vein in his neck pulsed wildly, and she wondered if he was having a stroke. Though she tried not to wish others harm, she couldn't help feeling that it would serve Chuck right if he did. He wanted what the Judge had. It seemed only right that he die the same way.

"I'm sorry for you."

"Don't be." A snarl had turned the face she'd once thought of as kind into something she didn't recognize.

When the Jeep slowed down, she seized the opportunity to jump. It wasn't easy, hampered as she was with her bound hands and the bulky clothing she wore. She landed and sprang to her feet and ran. The knee-deep snow impeded her efforts, but she kept moving.

The farther she went, the deeper the snow grew. The roar of an engine from behind hastened her steps, but it did no good. Her thighs burned as she gave it all she had. Cold, exhaustion and shock had zapped her strength, but she refused to give up.

Chuck pulled the truck to a stop. He got out and leaned against the vehicle, waiting for her. "Might as well give it up."

When she fell, she tried to push herself up, but the cold was so intense that her muscles wouldn't work.

He yanked her up by her wounded arm. Such was the pain that she couldn't help crying out.

"Now get in the Jeep before I tie you to the bumper and drag you behind me." The gleam in his eyes told her he'd take pleasure in the act. She complied, and he strapped the seat belt around her.

Huddled in the corner, she tried to keep her teeth from chattering.

Her hat and gloves were scant protection against the cold, but Chuck wasn't allowing her even that and ripped them away.

"You won't be going anywhere now," he said, his voice a blend of glee and satisfaction. "No, sirree. You won't be going anywhere."

She hated the smug tone of his voice.

"I've got to hand it to you," he said. "You had me going when you brought Danny back. But you aren't as smart as you think you are. If you'd been smarter, you'd have done as you were told and handed over the drugs. But, no, you had to bring in that no-account Brady." Hatred seemed to drip from his words as he mentioned Luca.

"Rest now," he spat out. "You're gonna need it."

"Thanks for the tip." She eyed the handgun he wore at his hip. Could she somehow wrestle it away from him with her hands lashed together?

"Don't even think about it," he warned.

"What?"

"Taking my gun. I won't kill you, but I've got no problem putting a bullet in you."

His weapon wasn't particularly big, but it packed a powerful punch.

"Would you really shoot me?" she asked.

"Yeah. I would." Chuck didn't apologize for the answer. It was the tone of his voice more than the words themselves that sent a chill skittering down her spine.

Where was he taking her? There was nothing around, nothing but snow-covered ground for a considerable distance. This piece of land was on her property, but she rarely came here. The expanse of snow, wedding-dress white, blanketed the field. It should have been beautiful. But knowing that the snow concealed a drug runners' base turned that beauty into something ugly.

How had she not known what her land was being used for? How had the Judge not known? He had always kept a sharp eye on everything he considered his. Other thoughts crowded her mind. Had he known and turned a blind eye? Or—the unthinkable—had he known because he was in on it?

The idea speared her with a pain so intense that she nearly doubled over. She and her father had never been close. He had treated her as he would anything else he owned: use it up until it was worn out and then discard it. Now she knew Chuck would do the same. She'd bide her time, look for an opening.

Doing her best not to be obvious, she looked around for something she could use as a weapon—anything— but nothing presented itself. She still had her brain. She wouldn't allow him to beat her.

"You don't want to do this." Desperation coated her words, but she didn't care. She had to convince him to let her go. If she didn't... She didn't finish the thought, unwilling to put into words, albeit silent, what the cartel would do to her.

"Got no choice."

"There's always a choice."

He shook his head vehemently. "Not when it comes to dealing with the cartel. Those guys would chew me up and spit me out."

"And you want to let them do that to me? You can go to Luca. He'd help you. All you have to do is ask."

"Like I said. Got no choice."

"You're sick. Really sick." She let her gaze rake him with contempt. "If you thought Calvin Sloan would give you the ranch, then you were lying to yourself."

Despite everything, she felt sorry for Chuck and sent him a pitying look. "The Judge was probably having a fine ol' time laughing at you."

The ruthless expression in his eyes reminded her that she was at his mercy. It wouldn't do her any good to antagonize him further, so she shut up.

The trip to wherever he was taking her was over too quickly. The Jeep came to rest in what looked like an empty field. "Get out. You're gonna be the guest of honor at the party."

When she failed to move, Chuck pulled her from the seat, manhandling her when she tried to resist. "It'll be better for you if you don't fight," he said. "These guys? They like it when their prisoners fight. Gives them an excuse to rough them up. Plus, they just like knocking people around. Especially women."

She was through begging, but she couldn't resist spitting in his eye. He wiped the spittle from his face and glared at her. "If you were a man, I'd knock you flat for that. Seeing as you're a woman, though, I'll do this instead." He drew back his arm and backhanded her.

She staggered under the force of the blow and then rubbed her jaw where he had struck her. "Don't do me any favors."

He laughed. "I have to hand it to you. You're a fighter. Maybe you're more like your old man than you thought."

Three men seemed to appear from nowhere. Then she realized that they had come from a hidden staircase. One was the goon she'd sparred with on that terrible day when she'd learned that Danny had been taken.

"I told you that we would meet again." Meanness glittered in his eyes.

She lifted her gaze so that it bored into his, letting him know that she wasn't going to go easily. She wasn't going to just roll over and submit meekly to whatever he and his partners had in store for her.

Not by a long shot.

Luca and Harper were to have met in the library at noon to discuss additional security measures. When fifteen minutes had slipped by and she hadn't shown up, he figured she was caught up in another project. When fifteen minutes turned to thirty, a strong dose of impatience shot through him.

It wasn't like her to be late.

A check with Danny told him that she hadn't been with their son. He was curled up on the overstuffed sofa in the front room reading. Had Harper just needed time to herself to process all that had happened in the last few days and taken off by herself? He rejected that idea immediately. She wouldn't have worried Danny and him that way.

Impatience took a hard turn to worry, and a sense of danger crowded his thoughts.

Where was she?

Luca reviewed the events of the day, trying to make sense of Harper's disappearance. Nothing suspicious. Nothing out of place. No outside vehicles in or out. Still, he knew something was wrong. The air reeked of it, and his skin crawled.

He enlisted help from the ranch hands and instructed them to check the outlying pastures and the outbuildings. Another thought intruded upon his mind, this one more chilling than any of the previous ones.

Had someone taken her?

If so, how had they gotten onto the ranch and then out again without notice? The security measures he'd installed made that unlikely. Fast upon the heels of that thought came another. Unless they had help from the inside. Harper had always denied that, but now he wasn't so sure.

He tromped through the snow looking for drag marks or signs of a struggle. He found plenty of footprints but nothing to indicate that something or someone had been dragged through the snow. Whoever took her wouldn't have had to drag her. She was small enough that the kidnapper could easily have slung her over his shoulders and carried her.

The sensation of danger should have abated after he'd checked on Danny a second time, but it only grew. Danny was safe, so why were the threads of fear pulling tighter around his neck?

He finally accepted what he'd already known. It hadn't been Danny who was the target. It was Harper. That took him full circle back to why she had been chosen in the first place to retrieve the drugs.

He had a feeling that if he could find the motive, it would

go a long way to helping him find Harper as well. The two of them had gone over anyone who might harbor resentment against her. The Judge had not been well-liked, but Harper was gaining a reputation in the mountain community as someone to be counted on.

He knew it wasn't the cartel that had taken her. The ranch was locked down so tight that a prairie dog couldn't get through. No, it had to have been someone closer.

He had run a thorough background search on everyone at the ranch, including the part-timers hired to help deliver feed to the stock during the winter. Nothing had stood out. There'd been a couple of DUIs and one barroom brawl, but otherwise, the ranch hands were clean. He'd had S&J's computer guru do the same and had gotten the same results.

When Tommy Shawcroft, a young ranch hand, ambled by, Luca stopped him. "You seen Dawson lately?" he asked.

Tommy scrunched up his face in a frown. "No, sir. Not since he sent me to the north pasture to check on some downed fences." He scratched his head. "Funny thing, though, there weren't no fences down. Guess Chuck was wrong."

"Guess so."

That wasn't like the foreman to make that kind of mistake. The ranch was short-handed as it was, and with the days darkening so early in the evening, they couldn't afford to have men waste time.

"You want I should tell him that you're looking for him?" Tommy asked.

"No, thanks." Luca hunched deeper into his coat, trying to ward off the wind that whipped through the ranch yard.

He went in search of Dawson but didn't find him anywhere. Luca frowned. The foreman was supposed to be overseeing the installation of additional cameras in the barn and other outbuildings. Nor could he find Harper after all this time searching.

Where is she?

The question fired through his mind with relentless persistence while a dark cloud of foreboding sat heavily over his head. Although nothing had changed from the time he'd last seen her until now, Luca knew that she was in trouble.

When it became apparent that Harper wasn't anywhere on the ranch and that her cell phone had been turned off, Luca knew he couldn't keep the truth from Danny any longer. The boy was old enough to understand that his mother was in danger.

Luca found Danny still curled up on the sofa in the front room. Using plain language, Luca told him the truth.

"Son, I've got hard news. News about your mother."

Danny straightened. "Did the bad guys get her?" The boy's calm earned Luca's admiration.

"How do you know?"

"Because she'd be here with me if she could."

The straightforward answer delivered in an equally straightforward way told Luca that Danny had his mother's strength and forthright honesty. His son didn't cry. Instead, he squared his small shoulders, reminding Luca of Harper.

"How do we get her back?" Danny asked.

"I'm working on that. Right now, I don't know where she is."

"Chuck can help. He knows his way around the mountains almost as good as my mommy does."

The foreman hadn't been around for most of the day, causing Luca to wonder where he'd been.

"Do you know where he is?" Luca asked.

Danny shook his head.

Interesting. It might not be a bad idea to hunt up Dawson and see if he had any ideas about who could have taken Harper. "I think I'll have a talk with him."

Danny jumped up. "Can I come with you?"

"Not this time," Luca said gently.

"I want to help get Mommy back."

"I know. I know." He thought for a moment. "There is something you can do for your mom."

"What's that?"

"Pray for her."

Danny sent him a curious look. "Do you believe in prayer?"

Luca thought on it.

"Will you say a prayer with me right now?" Danny asked. "For Mommy?"

Luca nodded. Maybe praying with Danny was the impetus he needed to reclaim his belief.

They knelt side by side and, despite feeling incredibly awkward, Luca uttered the first prayer to cross his lips in too many years.

ELEVEN

Chuck rushed her down a set of cement steps and then shoved her forward. Harper had finally figured out where she was. Decades ago, the government had built bunkers in various parts of the area and later closed them. This had to be one of those abandoned bunkers.

"Let me introduce you to El Jefe, otherwise known as Senor Delgado."

El Jefe stuck out a hand and cupped her chin.

"Look who we have here. The little lady who thought she and her partner could cheat us of what was ours." His mouth twisted into a parody of a smile. "Not feeling so smart now, are you?"

Knowing anything she said would enrage him, she kept her mouth shut.

"Nothing to say? C'mon. Tell me what you think of me. Where I come from, I am considered…how do you say it…a good catch."

Chuck had remained silent until now. Now he pushed himself forward. "I was promised fifty thousand dollars for my part. After that, I'm out."

The bravado of his words didn't match the fear glittering in his eyes. He was afraid of El Jefe. She didn't blame him. The organization's boss wasn't a large man, but he gave off the kind of vibes that made you want to put a whole lot of space between him and you, the kind that said he'd inflict pain for the sheer pleasure of doing so. She ought to know. She'd just been a victim of his brand of cruelty.

She wanted to tell him to forget about the money and get out of there. There was no way El Jefe would come through with the promised money. He had used Chuck and now no longer had any need for him.

However, it seemed that both she and El Jefe had under-estimated the foreman.

"I know what you're thinking," Chuck told the boss. "You're planning on getting rid of me. I kinda thought you would. That's why I left a letter with a lawyer in town if something happens to me."

El Jefe reared back his head and laughed. "You are not as dumb as you look. Do not worry. You will go free. But as for the money, you will not get it. What will you do? Go to the law? I do not think so."

Chuck's face turned an ugly purplish red, causing Harper to wonder if he was having a heart attack. Or a stroke. The color subsided, and, without another word, he left.

Delgado fixed a hard gaze on Harper. "Now you will tell me where my drugs are."

"I don't have them."

"Tell me or I will hurt you in ways you've never been hurt before."

She shook her head. "They're in the hands of the Feds."

For a second, El Jefe looked as apoplectic as Chuck had. "You will regret that." He raked her with an expression that promised retribution before turning to his men.

"Leave the woman alone. We may have need of her. Later, you can do what you want with her."

Murmuring rippled through the men, but no one made a move toward her, and she gave thanks for that.

She braced herself for what was coming. She would get through this, she promised herself. No matter what.

"Later," he said. "Later we will play a game." With those words he left.

Luca felt lost, like he was wandering around in a snow-storm with no sense of direction. For maybe the first time in his career, he doubted himself. He was second-guessing everything he did.

Why hadn't he better protected Harper? He'd known that the cartel wanted payback, and though he'd installed the best security available, he should have been more diligent at watching over her and stuck to her like white on rice.

Like that would have worked. He could only imagine her reaction if he'd tried following her around every min-ute of the day. But the excuse fell flat. He'd let her down in the worst way. Now he had to get her back.

Someone from the inside was aiding the enemy. But who?

When the answer came, he knew it was right. Chuck had been strangely unenthusiastic about Danny's homecom-ing and Harper's rescue. Luca had chalked it up to Vera's death and the man's habitual reticence, but, looking back, he could see it was more.

The why wasn't hard to figure. Money. Lots and lots of money. The cartels were known for having millions of dol-lars at their disposal.

After checking that Danny was in his room, Luca started toward the barn and ran into Tommy on the way. If the foreman wasn't there, Luca vowed to turn over every rock in Colorado to find him and discover what he'd done with Harper.

"Have you found Miss Harper yet?" the young ranch hand asked.

"Not yet." Luca continued on his way before he stopped and turned around. "Do you like the foreman?"

Tommy scuffed his boot in the dirty snow. "I guess he's okay."

"Anything about him seem off to you lately?"

Another scuff of boots. "Not really."

Luca picked up on the hesitation in the words. "What do you mean 'not really'?"

"Some of the men were surprised at the way he carried on at his missus's service. Word around the bunkhouse was that he was seeing a lady in town every Saturday night. I mean, why would he be so broken up about his missus being dead if he had someone on the side?" Tommy gnawed on his lower lip.

Why indeed?

Tommy pushed his tongue between his teeth. "Is that all?"

"Yeah. Thanks."

With that new information to chew on, Luca resumed his trip to the barn, where he found the foreman working on repairing tack. He approached quietly, wanting to take the man by surprise. "Hey there, Chuck."

After an initial pause, Dawson kept working. "You want something?" he finally asked.

"I'm worried about Harper. It's been over eight hours since anyone's seen her."

"Yeah?"

"Yeah. You know anything about it?"

Dawson merely shrugged, his back to Luca.

"Turn around," Luca ordered and trained his weapon on the foreman.

Dawson did as instructed, his expression one of surprise, then of consternation when he saw the weapon. "What's with the gun?"

His bewilderment appeared genuine, so much so that Luca was tempted to believe it, but there was something in the foreman's eyes, a glint of fear perhaps, that kept Luca holding the gun on him.

He ignored Dawson's question and asked one of his own. "Where's Harper? You were the last one seen with her."

"I don't know what you're talking about. Sure, Harper and I were together checking out a horse, but that was hours ago. Why would I know where she is now? She's a big girl. She can take care of herself."

It was an odd comment, given the circumstances.

When Luca didn't respond, Dawson rushed in with a spate of words. "I've been nothing but a friend to Harper and to Danny."

"Have you?" Luca let the question stand.

"Sure, I have. Ask anyone around here."

"That's strange, because from what I've seen, you've been pretty cold to her and Danny since they've been back."

Dawson's gaze turned hard, but he kept his peace.

Luca gave a harsh laugh. "Funny that you didn't immediately deny it."

For a minute, Luca thought Dawson was going to brazen it out, but then he smirked.

"You've got no proof that I did anything to her." Satisfaction filled the man's voice; at the same time, a smirk flirted with his mouth.

Luca bit down on his tongue in an effort to rein in his anger. If he focused on that pain, he might be able to think rationally. It turned out that rational wasn't in his wheel-house when it came to protecting Harper.

"Let me see your phone."

The smirk disappeared, and the glint of fear in the foreman's eyes intensified. "You've got no right."

Luca searched Dawson's pockets and came away with the phone. "Who am I gonna get when I punch the first number?"

Dawson tried to snatch the phone back.

"What did you do with her?" Right now, Luca was ready to take the foreman's head off. He contented himself by grabbing up a fistful of Dawson's jacket and yanking him off his feet. He let the man dangle there for a minute. The foreman's florid face drained of color, leaving only a mask of hatred mixed with a healthy dose of fear.

None too gently, Luca set Dawson back on his feet.

The older man inhaled sharply. "You near choked me to death."

"Don't tempt me. I'll ask you for the last time, what did you do with Harper?"

"What I had to." There was no apology in the older man's voice. Only cold pride.

"What does that mean?"

"It means I gave her to the people you cheated out of what was theirs."

"You took her to the cartel?" Luca could barely get the words out.

"You have something they want. Figure it out for yourself." There was no apology in Dawson's voice. Only cold satisfaction.

What kind of man took satisfaction in kidnapping a woman and turning her over to an organization as filthy as a cartel? "You must be feeling good about yourself right about now."

"I feel just fine."

"If something happens to Harper, I'm gonna make you wish you'd never been born."

"You won't." Dawson's smugness grated on Luca. "You're some law-enforcement big shot. You can't kill me."

"I'm not law enforcement. I work for a security firm. If my people found out what you did, they'd feel the same way I do."

The foreman no longer looked quite so smug. "What're you gonna do?"

"I'm waiting for you to tell me where Harper is. After that, we'll see."

"There's nothing but trouble for me if I tell you where she is."

Luca's free hand formed a fist. "There's nothing but trouble for you if you don't."

"I need time to think on it."

"Harper doesn't have time."

Dawson's face lost its ruddiness. In fact, he looked pale. "Tell me," Luca urged. "It'll go better for you if you do."

"I need that in writing."

"You know I don't have the authority to make a deal."

"Then find somebody who does 'cause I'm keeping quiet until I get something for my trouble."

It was all Luca could do not to slam his fist into the man's mouth.

Dawson must have felt Luca's anger for he hurried on with an explanation. "When you made off with the cocaine, the cartel wanted blood. Mine. I wasn't going to let them cut me into bits and pieces, not when it wasn't my fault that they didn't get their drugs." He hitched his chin. "It was you who done that. You and Harper. It was only fitting that she pay the price."

Luca made a move toward the foreman before reminding himself that he needed answers. He wasn't going to get them if he beat the man senseless. Aside from that practical matter, he didn't think he could fight a man who had thirty or more years on him. His code of honor wouldn't permit it. But, oh, how he was tempted.

He didn't have a problem admitting that he had the occasional issue with anger, especially when those he loved were threatened.

"I'll ask you a final time. Where is she?"

Dawson's smirk ignited Luca's temper. Cupping his hand, he smacked the man on the right side of the head. Though it looked like a fairly mild slap, it forced a painful stream of pressurized air into the ear canal, resulting in dizziness and even nausea.

Luca had picked up the technique when he was deployed. It was a useful move on a couple of counts. It didn't break any bones in the hand the way a punch could, and it didn't leave any marks.

He nearly spat the words out. "Start at the beginning. You turned her over to the cartel?"

"I had to. They were expecting it. If I hadn't…" Dawson made a chopping motion "…they'd slice and dice me until I'd be begging them to kill me. You know the score."

"Yeah, I know the score. I also know what they'll do to her."

The foreman merely lifted a shoulder in a careless shrug, once again threatening Luca's wrath. He'd already wrestled with his conscience over that, but restraint didn't come any easier at Dawson's nonchalance about Harper's fate.

"You'd have done the same," the foreman excused himself. "You don't want to mess with those guys."

"You're going to jail. I'll make sure of it. The only question is how long you'll be in for. If you don't help me now, I'll do my best to see that you spend the rest of your days behind bars." He let that sink in. "You'll die without ever setting foot outside prison walls again."

"You've got nothing on me. No one knows I was part of the kidnapping."

"*I* know."

"And who's going to believe you, the father of the kidnapped boy? I don't think so. Especially when I spread it around that you abandoned his ma before he was even born. No one's gonna feel sorry for you, much less believe you."

Luca didn't bother answering that. He was too busy thinking of what to do next. What *could* he do? He didn't have the cocaine anymore. It had been turned over to the DEA.

He grabbed Dawson by the collar of his coat and pushed him forward. "Walk."

"What're you gonna do to me?" The foreman's whine grated on his nerves.

Luca didn't know. If he had his way, he'd make good on the image in his mind of beating the man senseless, but that would bring only fleeting satisfaction and wouldn't help Harper.

"Do you have the number of your contact in your phone?"

Dawson lifted his chin. "You mess with the cartel, and you're asking to get killed."

"Maybe. Maybe not. But I'm not letting Harper be killed." Or worse. The *or worse* filled his mind with images that made him sick. He forced down the bile that swelled in his throat.

Resentfully, the foreman pulled his phone from his pocket, scrolled through the screen, showed it to Luca. "There. You happy?"

"I'm so far from happy and..." Luca didn't finish. "If I find you lied to me, you'll be breathing out of a tube for the rest of your life."

"You're a real piece of work, Brady."

"No. A real piece of work is a man who'd turn a helpless woman over to men intent on torturing and then killing her. Now give me the phone."

Harper hadn't slept. Couldn't. Her captors would be coming for her soon. The dark narrow room where she'd been taken didn't provide any amenities but for a thin mattress on a wire frame and a bucket.

She understood that she was a bargaining chip. When she was no longer useful, she would be killed. There had to be some way she could help herself. She wasn't one to sit around and wait for someone else to rescue her.

She knew Luca would be looking for her. She also knew he would have no idea of where to find her. He didn't even know that Chuck was involved. What if he left Danny with Chuck? What if her son was in danger again? Her heart rate kicked up, the blood pulsing through her veins. She had to find a way out of here...but how?

She thought maybe she'd gotten an answer when the same girl who had brought her food at the tent camp entered with a tray of food.

"Can you help me?" Harper asked her, desperation in her voice. "You know what they—" she gestured with a flick of her hand "—will do to me."

The girl gazed down at her feet. "The men will kill me. The only reason I am here is because my brother is one of them."

"Surely he'll protect you."

"No. He brought me here because our parents could no longer afford to feed me. But I am a prisoner as much as you." She set the tray on a rough table. "I wish I could help, but I cannot. I pray that these bad men will be captured, but I can do nothing."

Despite her own situation, Harper couldn't help but feel sympathy for the young girl. "I'm sorry."

The dark-haired girl shook her head. "Do not be sorry for me. It is you who you should be sorry for. The men plan bad things for you."

Harper could only too well imagine.

"I will return for your dishes." With that, the girl slipped out of the room, leaving Harper to ponder her fate. She discovered she was hungry and started on the meal. She used her fingers as there were no utensils, probably because they could be turned into weapons.

To her surprise, she ate every bite and found herself wishing for more. Who knew when they would feed her again or how long she'd be a prisoner here? The possible scenarios were so frightening that she wanted to curl up into a ball and hide in the oblivion of sleep.

Disgusted by where her thoughts were leading, she pushed the tray away. That wasn't like her. She looked around, assessing what she could use for a weapon. The room was empty but for the mattress on its wire frame. Nothing there.

Or was there?

She lifted the mattress off the bed frame and saw what she wanted. Metal hooks that linked the bed frame together.

Painstakingly, she undid each hook from its neighbor and then cradled them in her palm as though they were gold. Hastily, she put the bed back together as best she could and then started on the task of straightening the hooks. The bed was old and cheap, as were the hooks. Bending them didn't require as much strength as she feared, and soon she had all ten done. She placed them between her fingers and smiled grimly to herself. They would do nicely as a weapon.

You can do this.

Of course, she could. On one search-and-rescue mission, she'd been trapped on a mountain ledge with nothing but her wits and what she carried in her backpack, including grappling hooks, a length of rope and an ice saw. Using them, she had gotten herself off the ledge and rescued the missing child while she was at it.

A scripture from Proverbs appeared in her mind. *The wicked flee when no man pursueth: but the righteous are bold as a lion.* She repeated that to herself when she heard a fumbling at the door. She flattened herself against the wall behind the door. When it opened, she heard a grunt of surprise when the guard stared at what appeared to be an empty room.

He ventured in enough to where Harper could launch her attack. She jumped him, wrapping her arms around his neck and drew her newly acquired claws down his neck. He gave a satisfying howl of surprise as she dug the springs into the fleshy jowls of his throat. Blood streaked down his neck, but he didn't stop to wipe it away.

He flung her off, bared his teeth and aimed a Mossberg at her head. She wasn't overly familiar with the Mossberg pistol, but she knew enough to recognize the MC2SC model and knew it carried a double-stack eleven and fourteen round magazine. Though it was slim and compact, it packed a wallop.

A moment later, she noticed the metal gleaming on his other hand. Brass knuckles. She had no experience with them but knew they could break bones if applied with enough force.

First, though, she had to deal with the deadly looking gun. She spun and kicked the weapon from his hand. It landed with a clatter on the floor. As she bent and closed her hand around its butt, he clipped her in the jaw with his fist. Pain seared through her as the knuckles connected with skin and flesh.

Dizzy, she lost her grip on the gun. It went flying, landing somewhere behind her. Her foe was already on her and delivered a savage blow to her stomach, forcing the air from her lungs. He followed up by delivering a hard kick to her face. The crunch of bone told her that he'd probably broken her nose. The metallic taste of blood filled her mouth.

Still reeling from that, she was unable to avoid a second kick, this one to her gut. She doubled over but refused to cry out. When she fell to the ground, he kicked her again and again. In the ribs, chest and head. Her vision blurred, and her ears rang.

She wasn't alone. The Lord was on her side, and she prayed for His protection, asking for strength to withstand the brutal treatment.

"What's it gonna take to make you beg?"

The final time, she couldn't keep from crying out. Her lungs were on fire with pain. "Are you satisfied?" she asked when she got her voice back.

"Not hardly."

"You're a pitiful excuse for a man." Her words were

slurred, and she wouldn't be surprised to learn she had a couple of broken teeth.

He yanked her to her feet.

She couldn't let him get in another strike. Blinking against the white lights exploding inside her head, she marshaled all her strength and pistoned a knee to his groin. His yell of outrage bounced off the walls of the small room.

He wheezed out a mighty *oomph* and gave her a look of pure hatred before collapsing to the floor.

Fighting to remain conscious, she didn't have time to gloat. She dove on top of him and pulled the brass knuckles from his hand. It was no easy task as he fought her every inch of the way, but eventually she managed to get them off him and slipped them on her own hand.

"Let's see how you like it." She slammed her fist into his face, his neck, his gut. With every punch, he gave a satisfying grunt.

She didn't let up until he had stopped struggling. She hadn't killed him, but she'd made him hurt. That was good enough. She spotted a length of leather woven through his long braid. She pulled it out and tested it. Though thin, it was sturdy. She tied it around his wrists then undid his belt and bound his ankles. For good measure, she took a stained kerchief from around his neck and stuffed it in his mouth.

She sat back and tried to catch her breath. Every inch of her hurt. If she came out of this with only a few broken ribs, she'd consider herself fortunate. She tucked the Mossberg at her waist; the knuckles, she put in her pocket.

When she felt able to stand, she struggled to her feet. Recalling the vicious licks the man had given her, she reared back her leg and kicked him in the gut. It was probably petty to take satisfaction in his *oomph* of pain, but she couldn't help it.

Even without words, he managed to convey his hatred, and she knew she would be in for a bad time if he ever got his hands on her again.

She'd have to make certain that that didn't happen. In the meantime, there were still at least three more guards, plus the boss, El Jefe.

Think.

She knew Luca would move heaven and earth to find her, but would he remember the long-ago conversation when she'd told him how the area had once been a government bunker complete with a stockpile of weapons, nonperishable foods and other goods? She had nearly forgotten it herself.

The door burst open. The man whose shoulder she'd twisted stood there, a long, serrated knife in his hand. He turned it back and forth, metal gleaming even in the stingy light given off by the room's single bulb.

Fear-fueled adrenaline surged through her. *Use it*, she told herself. *Use it and survive.*

TWELVE

It was time to stop wallowing in a mire of self-imposed guilt.

Luca knew he needed help and called fellow ex-ranger and S&J operative Matt Hensley. "I need a location from a phone number. Can you set me up?"

"It may take a little time," Matt said.

"Time is something I don't have." Luca gave a rundown of what was happening.

A sharply indrawn breath was Matt's response. "I'll rush the search on the location. How about I come and provide backup?"

"There's nothing I'd like better. If you can round up a couple of brothers, I'd be obliged."

"Will do. They'll jump at the chance to mix it up with cartel members."

"Thanks, man. You're the best."

Luca had thought of calling in the Feds, but he knew their primary focus would be on stopping the flow of drugs through the area rather than saving Harper. While he understood their goal, he needed people he could count on to get her to safety.

Thirty minutes later, Matt called back with the info on the address. Luca entered it in his phone, did a search for it. When he had it, he nodded to himself. He had a place to start.

One more thing to take care of. He'd told Tommy to lock Dawson in an outbuilding. He had no idea how long he would be gone, and he wasn't taking any chances with Danny's safety. He called Ginny Robinson and explained the circumstances. Not only was she a first-rate nurse and security professional, Danny knew her and would be reassured by her presence.

"I'm on my way," she said. "Be there in an hour." True to her word, Ginny arrived within the hour. "Don't worry," she said. "I'll take care of him as if he were my own son."

Luca had never been so glad to see anyone in his life as he was when Matt, Brett Overcash and Nash Reynolds showed up. Ready for action, they were dressed in Nomex snowsuits, Oakley shades and kick-in-the-door army boots. Each carried an array of weapons that, along with the determined expressions on their rugged faces, had Luca almost feeling sorry for the men who held Harper.

Almost.

Often, when members of the armed services, especially special operators, returned home, they found that they had no place in society. The skills the military had spent millions of dollars in training on were of no value in the workplace.

S&J Security/Protection and other companies like it had changed that, offering jobs where veterans could use their special skills and help others at the same time. For those accustomed to serving their country and their fellow man, it was the perfect job after leaving the military.

"Got the rest of our gear in the truck," Matt said. "I put Brett in charge." In their unit, Brett was known as the "scavenger." If he couldn't get it, it wasn't worth getting.

Brett now gave a toothy grin. "You know I don't go no-where without my babies." He lifted an AR15 from the back seat and stroked it lovingly.

Brett had made an excellent quartermaster overseas. He brought those same skills now. The bed of the truck held helmets, night-vision goggles, a thermal scope, a hand-held drone, encrypted radios and a SERE kit. Each of them was well-trained in SERE—survival, evasion, resistance and escape. In addition to the weapons, there were tactical gloves, chem lights and battle belts with holsters designed especially for a Glock.

Luca gave a short nod of thanks. He didn't bother asking where Brett had picked up the truckload of toys. The spec op community was a small but helpful one. For what he couldn't get from S&J, he had friends who could lay their hands on most anything needed for combat.

These were men and women who held country and flag dear. None tolerated those who preyed on the weak and innocent. And though Harper wasn't weak and had seen enough of the world to no longer be innocent, she was a woman. Rangers, ex or not, didn't take kindly to men who abused women.

Matt and the two other ex-rangers from their unit in Af-ghanistan had joined S&J in the last three years. The four of them had seen plenty of action in the Stand and wanted to continue the good fight when they returned home.

There was one more operative. Stacy Rendell. Stacy was ex-CIA and had worked as an SSO or specialized skills of-ficer. She was a top-notch marksman who could outshoot the rest of the team. It didn't hurt that she was easy on the eyes and smart as a whip, making her a first-rate operative when it came to obtaining information.

Luca held out a hand. "Stace. Glad to have you on board."

"You didn't think I was going to let these yahoos—" she gestured to Matt and the others "—have all the fun, did you?" She took his hand with a grip that belied her small size. More soberly, she added, "When Matt told me what was going on, I volunteered."

Luca knew she'd lost her younger brother to a drug overdose. She had made no secret of her contempt for anyone in the drug trade.

"I appreciate it. This isn't gonna be a walk in the park. The men who have Harper fight dirty."

She bared her teeth. "Good. There's nothing I like better than getting down and dirty with the enemy." She patted the Colt holstered at her waist. "I won't let you down."

"I know."

With four highly trained operatives having his back, Luca felt like the odds of getting Harper back had improved exponentially.

"What're our ROE?" Stacy asked, referring to the rules of engagement.

"If you see someone with a weapon, shoot first and ask questions later. The enemy we're facing has a first-rate arsenal. Maybe even better than what Brett brought. They fight mean, and they fight dirty."

"We'll be ready," Matt said. "Let 'em bring it."

Luca wanted to say something, but he didn't have words. Except one. "Thanks."

This team was the only way to get Harper back alive.

A heavy hand clamped on Harper's shoulder. "You thought you could get away?" The man spat on the floor. "Stupid woman."

Her heart sank. She'd been so close.

He pushed her back inside the cell. "I see you've been

busy," he said with a glance at the still unconscious man on the floor. Her tormentor kicked the man. "Get up."

The other man stirred, made a mumbling sound.

"What kind of man are you to be taken down by a woman?"

His gaze shot daggers of hate at her as he was subjected to the humiliation of having the other man undo the bindings of his hands and feet.

Great. Now she had two men who wanted revenge on her.

The two men began talking in Spanish, obviously believing that she wouldn't understand. Though she couldn't pick up everything, she caught enough to realize that they were planning on killing her before they folded up the operation here. Unfortunately, that didn't tell her anything she hadn't already guessed.

"You will be sorry you stole from us," the first man said.

"Sorry I kept drugs from being sold to children?" She imitated him and spat, narrowly missing his boots. "I don't think so."

He looked like he wanted to strangle her then and there.

Arguing over who would get to kill her when El Jefe gave the word, the men left.

Harper stomped her feet on the ground, anything to restore the circulation in them. She had stopped feeling the cold, a sign, she knew, of hypothermia. In a way, it was a relief, but she understood the danger. Her arms and legs felt heavy now, along with her eyelids, tempting her to give in to the oblivion of darkness.

No! She couldn't succumb to the desire to curl up and go to sleep. It wasn't in her to give up, and it frightened her that she'd even considered it.

With a fierceness borne of faith and stubbornness, she gave everything she had to stay awake. She thought of

Danny and how scared he must be to know that she was missing. She would get through this for him.

She had to.

With renewed determination, she forced herself to walk the short distance across the room and back again. Over and over. So far, she was safe, as El Jefe had told the guard to keep his hands off her, but that wouldn't last for long. Once he learned that Luca didn't have the drugs, that they'd been handed over to the Feds, he would order her death. A very painful death, she feared.

She refused to give up. She hadn't yet told Luca that she loved him, had never stopped loving him, even during the intervening years when she'd believed that he'd stopped caring about her.

She loved him. He and Danny gave her reason to stay alive, and stay alive, she would.

"What's the plan?" Matt asked after Luca ushered the team to the study, where he had laid out a map of the area on the desk.

Luca pointed to the location the call was made from. "I'm thinking they have a warehouse or something from which they operate. It's the only thing that makes sense. They can't cut cocaine from a hut or tent. They need a place where they can process it."

"How could they keep that on the DL from everyone?" Brett asked.

That was something Luca had pondered. With Dawson in their pocket, they had an edge. Still, though, they'd need a place that wasn't immediately visible from the ground or the air. Unless…

He recalled the clay that had coated the boots of the

men he'd tangled with. Had they built a compound *under-ground*?

He rejected the idea immediately. There was no way such a thing could be constructed without attracting unwanted attention. Not to mention, the frigid weather would make such an undertaking impossible.

But with Dawson's guidance, they could have found a place that didn't attract attention. Luca voiced his thoughts aloud.

"There's one more thing," he added. "Looks like the cartel has partnered up with terrorists."

A grim silence settled over the small group as each recognized the significance of the news.

"If you want out…" Luca began.

Matt cut him off. "We're here, and we're sticking. We'll get your lady back and then make sure the men who took her live to regret it."

Though Luca wanted to repeat his earlier thanks, he only gave a short nod and went to work. Special operators didn't get emotional, even when their brothers—and that went for Stacy as well—put it all on the line for them. He met each of their gazes with an unflinching one of his own, one that said everything.

They knew he'd do the same for them. Each of them had gone to the mat for the others multiple times on S&J missions or in the Stand. Nothing had changed.

It promised to be a rough trip, one he didn't know he'd return from, but Harper needed him. That said it all.

Luca and his team made the first part of the journey by snowmobile. When the vehicles could no longer make it, the team dismounted and began the arduous trek on foot.

Luca called a break two hours into the trek. Though all five were in excellent physical condition, the altitude with its thin air and the extreme cold diminished their oxygen intake.

"Drink some water," he said. Hydrating was crucial. It didn't matter that the temperature hovered only a few degrees above zero. No one could sustain the energy they were expending without replenishing fluids. They chowed down on energy bars and chocolate. Nobody spoke, each too intent on getting enough fuel into their bodies for what lay ahead.

Thoughts of Harper crowded his mind. What was she going through? His fists tightened at the idea of any of the cartel members harming her. Whether they had a future together or not, he would never stop caring about her.

With break time over, they checked and rechecked equipment. As far as Luca was concerned, you couldn't check your weapons and gear enough. A faulty trigger or a jammed gun barrel could make the difference between life and death.

That done, they resumed the journey. Deep pockets of gloom had taken shape between the trunks of trees so wide that it would take two or more men to span their circumference. A dense canopy overhead all but erased the last vestiges of light. An hour later, they neared the area Matt had identified as the probable location of the bunker.

Luca offered his teammates one last opportunity to bow out. "No one's gonna think less of you if you decide to sit this one out," he said. "I don't know how many bogies we'll be facing. The only thing that I know for sure is that they'll be out for blood." With all the unknowns, the mission could easily go south. He was all in to risk his life for Harper, but he couldn't expect his buddies to risk theirs.

No one took him up on it.

Brett slapped him on the back. "Let's get to it."

Fifteen minutes later, Luca held up a fist, signaling that they needed to maintain silence from here on out.

He had no doubts about the courage and ability of the four comrades with him. With only five members of the team, though, they were seriously outnumbered.

They stopped at the edge of the thickly wooded forest, hiding in a tangle of undergrowth, the branches of a huge spruce further deepening the darkness of the area. His ears listened to detect even the slightest sound. Within a few minutes, he could distinguish the difference between a small animal scampering through the snow and the rustle of the wind in the branches. He motioned for Brett and Nash to flank the east side, while he and Matt took the west. Recon played a large part in whether you won or lost a battle, whether you lived or died.

With his night vision goggles, he spotted a small building. It wasn't nearly large enough to contain a drug operation, but it might be an outbuilding. "We start here," he told his teammates.

"Stace, find a spot where you can see who's coming and going. Let us know when you see movement."

Nimbly, Stacy scrambled up the trunk of a pine.

"You have it bad for the lady," Matt said in a low voice, his breath coming in plumes of wispy white.

Luca didn't pretend that he didn't know what his friend was talking about and saw no reason in denying it. "I always have."

"She the one who got away?"

"Something like that."

"And the boy?"

"He's my son."

The three words filled him with something still new and wondrous. He had a son. Could he and Harper and Danny make a family? Or was it too late? He pushed the idea from his mind. First, he had to get her back.

Luca and Matt started searching. The opening couldn't be too obvious. At the same time, however, it had to be easily accessible.

Luca marked off a grid search and started at the north end.

Just when he decided he had it all wrong, he felt something different in the ground, a hard surface buried just beneath a layer of snow and dirt.

He signaled, and the others came running. Together, the four of them brushed away the snow and loose dirt. It appeared to be a modern version of a trapdoor, complete with noiseless hinges and a pressure plate that slid the door to the side.

"Door's moving," Stacy said over their coms.

"Good, copy," Luca replied.

No questions were asked. The men disappeared, melting out of sight.

When the door slid open, a man climbed out.

Luca let him get all the way out before wrapping his arm around the man's neck and applying enough pressure he couldn't escape, not if he wanted to keep breathing.

"I c...can't breathe," the man choked out.

Matt pulled Luca away and pushed the man to Brett, who was ready with flex-cuffs and a gag. Luca was ready to charge down the steps, find Harper and take out anyone who stood in his way.

Matt wrapped a hard hand around Luca's arm, restraining him. "Play it smart, man. First, we get the info and then we make our move. Not before."

Matt was right.

But Luca didn't want to wait. He jerked a thumb to a

thicket of brush and scraggly pine. "Take him over there." Luca fixed a hard gaze on the prisoner. "We'll get our info. One way or another."

Once they'd interrogated the man they'd pulled from the bunker and learned its setup, Luca was ready to go but for one thing.

"We need a diversion. Something to get the bogeys' attention while I get Harper out." He got a better look at the building he'd spotted earlier. From the shape and structure, it looked like it could be a weapons stockpile. It wasn't safe or practical to keep underground.

"Let's take a look," he said to Matt.

The two of them tramped through the snow and did a recon of the building. He'd been right—it was a stockpile of weapons. Everything from AR15s to rocket launchers to boxes of grenades.

"Blowing that up would make a right fine diversion," Matt said. He'd been the demolitions expert in the unit.

Luca signaled Nash and Brett to join them. "What do you think? Can you guys take it out?"

Matt was the first to speak. "Shucks. I can do that with one arm tied behind my back."

"The three of us can take it out without breaking a sweat," Brett said.

Nash rounded it out. "No problem."

Stacy had shimmied down the tree and now made it clear that she wasn't going to be left out. "And what do you think I'm going to be doing while you big strong men are having all the fun?"

"Okay, fine," Matt said with exaggerated patience. "You can come with us."

Luca looked at his teammates. "When this is over, I'm going to owe all of you the best steak dinner in Colorado."

Nash grinned. "Make that chili and dogs, and I'm in."

"You always were a class act," Stacy said.

The lighthearted banter felt good, but Luca didn't let it delude him into thinking that what came next would be easy. He stripped off his clothes, then, after undoing the guard's cuffs, did the same with him. He donned the guard's distinctive shirt and pants and a belt buckle the size of a man's fist.

Dressed in the guard's clothes, Luca hoped to pass for the other man.

"I'm going in. Give me thirty minutes and then light up the stockpile."

"You want we should go in after?" Brett asked.

"No. I want you to get out of here and don't look back."

Matt crossed his arms over his chest. "Not going to happen, man," he said, his voice as unyielding as his posture.

"Look, if Harper and I don't make it out…" he paused there "…there has to be someone left to show the authorities where the bunker is and to tell the story. I'm depending on you—" he included each of his team in his glance "—to do exactly that."

"One of us could do that," Matt protested. "It won't take all of us."

"I've already asked more of you than I had a right to. This isn't negotiable. Take off after you light it up."

It was Stacy who answered for all of them. "I didn't come here to turn tail and run if things got hairy. I came to get your lady and to take out drug runners, and that's what I'm going to do." She fixed a hard gaze on Luca. "No matter what."

Luca took in the mutinous looks on his friends' faces and reluctantly nodded.

Matt pulled him aside. "Want I should go down? As I recall, you and bunkers don't mix, man."

For one shaming moment, Luca was tempted to take his friend up on the offer. When he'd served in Afghanistan, he and his unit had located a warlord squirreled away in a bunker. All had gone well until one of his minions had tossed a grenade in the room. All but two of Luca's men had been killed. He'd never forgiven himself and had shied away from entering bunkers ever since.

"I haven't forgotten. Thanks, but no thanks. This is mine."

"I figured you'd feel that way." Matt clasped Luca's shoulder. "Go get your lady. We'll be waiting topside for you."

With his newly found belief in God, Luca prayed silently as he made his way down the stairway to the bunker.

He'd have been lying if he said he wasn't afraid as he descended into the darkness. Moreover, he'd have been foolish if he wasn't. Luca had never considered fear a weakness. It was what you chose to do with your fear that decided how you lived your life.

He was grateful that he'd *convinced* the man whose clothes he wore to give him a detailed description of what he'd find. After a sharp right, he followed a straight corridor until he reached the fourth door, and he mule-kicked it open.

What he saw inside sent a wave of fury through him. Harper was tied to a chair. One man bent over her, clearly ready to hit her with a knuckle-wrapped fist. Her face was bruised, and tears had left tracks down her cheeks. He wanted to gather her to him and promise that nothing would ever hurt her again, but first he had to take care of the man who'd been ready to use the knuckles on her.

Anger igniting his temper, Luca bolted in, yanked the

man off his feet and let him dangle in the air before throwing him to the ground.

"Why don't you pick on someone your own size?" He slammed his fist into the man's face.

First, he'd see to Harper. Then he'd finish what he started.

THIRTEEN

Luca had come, just as she'd known he would. Later, if they got out of this—no, *when* they got out of this—she'd ask how he found her. Right now, they had to concentrate on one thing and one thing only.

Surviving.

After dispatching the guard who had been interrogating her, he pulled the knife from the scabbard strapped to his left thigh and cut Harper loose, frowning at the sight of her reddened wrists.

"I'm okay," she said. Luca had risked his life to save hers. She couldn't let him waste it.

"I didn't come alone," he whispered. "I brought some friends along. They're waiting for us up top."

Movement through the open door snagged her attention. "Luca! Watch out!" Harper cried out as two goons pushed their way into the cell. One was big. The other, huge.

"Get out of here," Luca shouted at her and faced off with the larger of the two.

She ignored his command and turned her attention to the man who had tried to strangle her a week ago. Had it only been a week?

"I told you that we would meet again."

When he made his move, she was ready and blocked his

fist with her forearm. He knocked it aside easily, but she spun on her left foot and struck out with her right, catching him in the solar plexus.

"Nice," he said and licked his lips, clearly anticipating what came next.

She used her elbow to cuff his side. A little bit lower, and she would have gotten his kidney, a particularly vulnerable area. Next time. But she wasn't given a next time as he grabbed both of her wrists and locked them together in one large hand.

He moved easily for such a big man. There was no wasted energy.

She slid a glance at Luca, saw the larger man lunge at him. He dodged a punch and darted a glance her way. She winced when she saw his opponent land the next one, a blow to his jaw.

"I told you to get out of here," Luca yelled to her.

Once again, she ignored his order and kept raining down her fists on her attacker's head. She got in a good punch to his ears, but he shook her off, like a bad-natured bear swatting a pesky fly. She didn't stay down but got back up and struck out with her leg, tripping him. He landed with a thud. On the floor, he didn't look so intimidating. She stomped on his neck and ground her booted foot into the soft flesh.

Harper's opponent had good moves, and he managed to slide out from beneath her foot. Again, he advanced on her.

She fought with everything she had until her hands were hurting so badly she felt she couldn't use them any longer.

Still, she didn't give up.

When he wrapped thick-fingered hands around her neck, she had a flashback to a week ago when he'd tried to strangle her. She brought her knee up between their bodies and rammed it between his legs with all the force she could muster. His yowl of pain told her she'd done some damage.

Good.

He released her and clutched the tender area, rocking back and forth, giving her precious seconds to regroup, but time was against her, and her opponent, fury in his eyes, came at her once more.

She pivoted on her right foot, raised her left and kicked him at the side of his knee. His yowl of pain echoed off the rocks. People mistakenly thought the knee itself was the vulnerable area when, in fact, it was the side of the knee that held the most sensitive nerve. Before he could recover, she followed up with a second kick.

"Lady, you're gonna be real sorry you did that."

She smashed the heel of her hand into his nose. She didn't let up, even when he grabbed her wrist and tried to twist it away. Blood spurted from his nose, immediately covering his mouth and chin. He swiped at it but only succeeded in smearing it over his entire face.

While he ineffectually tried to clean the blood out of his eyes so that he could see, she sized up the situation.

Blood coated her hand, ran down her arm. When the man finally succeeded in pushing her away, she fell backward and hit her head with a hard thump.

She scrambled up, but, by that time, he'd grabbed hold of her upper arms. As she'd learned from her instructor, she brought her elbows together, breaking his hold.

The surprise on his face was almost comical. She used her freed hands to clap over his ears, resulting in a gratifying slap.

Her opponent yelped and grabbed his ears, staggering back. And Harper knew this was her chance, the moment that would decide her fate.

* * *

Luca eyed his foe, perhaps the largest man he'd ever seen, and knew he was in for the fight of his life. So he set his jaw and locked gazes with the man who topped his six-foot-three frame by nearly four inches. Luca drew his weapon, only to have it kicked from his hand. Before he could reach it, his opponent smashed his fist into Luca's face with the force of a battering ram.

The man angled his jaw. "Come on. I'll give you one free punch," he taunted. His eyes gleamed with eagerness and a large dose of arrogance to go along with it.

Luca didn't go for the punch. That was a sucker's move. Getting close enough to use his fists meant getting close enough that the man could take him out with one swipe of a huge hand, a hand that resembled a bear's paw. Instead, Luca pivoted then kicked out high with his right leg aiming for the man's kidneys.

The man's resounding *oomph* of pain was rewarding, but it wasn't going to keep him from mopping the floor with Luca if he didn't do something quick. He wasn't given time to ponder over it when the goon wrapped arms thick as trees around Luca's middle, lifting him off the ground as though he weighed nothing, and held him there. With his arms trapped against his sides, Luca should have been helpless, but he wasn't down yet. He reared back his head and rammed it into his opponent's face.

The crunch of bone against bone told him that he'd probably broken the man's nose. The spurt of blood confirmed his guess. His foe released him immediately and dropped Luca to the ground.

Luca didn't have time to catch his breath before his opponent was on him again, this time kicking him in the ribs. He tried to dance out of the way but wasn't quick enough.

It didn't take much to deduce he'd end up with a broken rib or two before this was over. He'd be fortunate if that was all he ended up with.

Still on the ground, he propped himself up on his elbows and struck out with his right leg, catching the man in the groin. It was a down-and-dirty move, one that had saved him in the past when he'd tangled with a larger opponent. Surprise mixed with a hefty dose of pain twisted his opponent's mouth into a snarl and caused him to double over in agony.

Luca hastily got to his feet.

Rage had darkened his adversary's eyes. Fisting meaty hands, he charged toward Luca.

Luca sidestepped. Unable to stop the momentum, the man lost his balance and toppled to the ground. Luca had the advantage now and intended on using it. While his opponent was still reeling with pain, Luca had time to grab his weapon. Outrage mixed with disbelief crossed his foe's face.

Luca guessed the big man wasn't accustomed to being bested. Under any other circumstances, his expression would be comical, a mixture of bewilderment and fury.

"Not so much fun taking on a man rather than a woman, is it?" he taunted.

Such a man would not take kindly to being the object of ridicule, and Luca grinned, letting his contempt show, hoping to incite his enemy's temper. "You look mighty funny with a smashed-in nose."

"I'll make you pay," the man ground out.

Luca decided to use that anger to his favor. When the man rushed him, Luca turned to the side, presenting a smaller target. With more force than reason, his opponent unleashed the full extent of his temper, causing him to run smack into the wall and then fall to the ground with a sat-isfying thump.

Luca turned him over, put a knee to his back and held him in place while securing his hands with a flex-cuff.

Harper glanced at Luca and saw that he was holding his own against the behemoth who used his fists like sledge-hammers, but his face was bloodied along with his own knuckles. How long could he hold out?

If something happened to him... She couldn't go there.

Before she could advance on her ailing opponent, he charged her again. She'd made a serious mistake. She'd failed to realize that her foe had only been playing with her. He came at her hard. Before she could stop him, he cir-cled his hands around her neck then squeezed. Her breath stalled, and she gasped as she struggled to break his grip. Blackness swirled before her eyes. In another thirty sec-onds, she knew she'd lose consciousness. From there, it would all be over.

Summoning her last ounce of strength, she raised her elbows horizontally to the top of her delts. A jab of hard bone against the soft tissue of the neck caught the man by surprise and threw him against the wall, then she drove a fist into his belly.

For a big man in otherwise good shape, he had a soft gut. He grunted as she ground her fist into it and kept grinding. When he dropped to the floor, she slammed her foot on his head, experiencing a jolt of satisfaction. It was short-lived, however, as she realized that though she'd scored a point, he wouldn't be caught by surprise a second time.

He reared up and grabbed her wrist. She wrenched free, but she was running out of strength. If he caught her again, she was done for.

He peeled back his lips in a parody of a smile. When he came at her again, he roared, teeth bared, eyes promising retribution. She danced out of his way, not easy in the narrow space. She knew she was no match for this bull of a man.

She pivoted on her right foot, raised her left and kicked him at the side of his knee. His scream echoed off the rocks. Before he could recover, she followed up with a second kick.

She spun and, using every last bit of strength she had left, caught him in the chest, sending him to the ground. She didn't waste the opportunity but jumped on him and pummeled him in the face with her fists.

He shook her off.

She came in from the side, aiming for the kidneys. She gave it everything she had and was gratified when he doubled over, making him vulnerable to an attack to the back of his neck.

She spared a glance at Luca and was not surprised to see that his opponent was also on the ground and that Luca was securing his hands with a flex-cuff.

She brought the side of her hand down with as much force as she could muster, sending her attacker to the floor, but he wasn't out. She jumped on top of him and put everything she had into keeping him from getting up.

Just when she knew she couldn't keep it up, Luca lifted her off the man. "You've done enough, tiger."

She hoped he was right, because she didn't think she had anything left in her.

The last of her strength had been spent.

Luca yanked the man she'd been battling to his feet and, grabbing his left arm, twisted it behind his back.

"You broke it. You broke my arm." The man whined like a baby denied his bottle. "C'mon, man. Let up."

"Men who beat up on women don't deserve any mercy in my book." Luca growled his displeasure as he looked at her bruised face, and she knew he was considering beating the man to a pulp.

"Not now, Luca," Harper said. "Let's get this one tied up."

With smooth efficiency, they bound her opponent's hands with flex-cuffs and then locked the two men inside a storage room.

By this time, Harper was struggling to put one foot in front of the other, and Luca slipped an arm beneath her shoulder and half carried, half lifted her from the room. She knew he would have carried her the entire way, but she refused.

"Thank you for coming," she said.

"Did you think I wouldn't?"

"No," she whispered. "I knew you'd come." A sweet feeling filled her, despite the cold, despite the pain radiating through her from the beating she'd taken, despite the danger they were still in. He'd risked his life to save hers. Again.

How could she ever thank him? Would he now walk out of her life? The idea left a hole in her heart that she doubted would ever be filled if he didn't stay.

He tapped the com attached to his collar. When a female voice answered, he said, "Package is secured."

"Good, copy."

She was beginning to think they might survive after all.

Within seconds, an explosion sounded. "That's our signal," Luca said and grabbed her hand. "My team just blew the arsenal."

"What now?" she asked, her voice rough with the exertion of battling the man who had threatened to slice her into pieces.

"We go up top and find my team."

It was then that she remembered the young girl who had been as much a prisoner as she had. "I have to find someone. A girl who's being held here."

"You need to get out of here. I'll send a couple of guys from my team back for her." Luca grabbed her hand and pulled her through the narrow passageway to the steps leading out of the bunker. As quickly as her tired, aching limbs permitted, she climbed the rungs. When she got to the top, she pushed against the door carved into the earth. It gave way.

She blinked against the sun. How long had she been in the bunker? It didn't matter. She was free now.

Free.

FOURTEEN

Stacy pumped a fist in the air. "We showed them."

"If I had lost you," Luca started.

Harper put a finger to his lips. "You didn't. You saved me. You're a knight in shining armor just like in Danny's book."

"I'm no knight. I'm just a guy who happens …" He stopped. He'd almost admitted that he loved her, that he had never stopped loving her. But now wasn't the time. Or the place. So he kept what he'd been about to say to himself.

He introduced Harper to the team, then aimed a narrow-eyed gaze at her, noting the multiple bruises on her face and neck. He had kept his arm around her shoulders and now also noticed that she was shivering uncontrollably. No wonder. She had to be nearly frozen to death from time in the bunker and now exposure to the below-freezing temperatures outside. He shrugged off his jacket and wrapped it around her.

"Can you guys button up here?" he asked. "I want to get Harper home." Rightfully, she should be in the hospital, but he doubted she'd agree.

"I'm all right," she protested. "We have to make sure that none of these goons escapes."

"They won't be going anywhere," Matt promised. "We'll make sure of it."

"There're more still down there, including two locked in a storage room." Luca jerked this thumb toward the bunker.

"One of them is El Jefe," Harper added. "He's not as big as some of his men, but he's twice as mean. We can't let him get away. And there's a young girl down there, as well. I expect she's hiding."

"We'll find her and take care of the rest of them," Stacy promised. Good to her word, she and Matt descended into the bunker. Five minutes later, they emerged with the remaining men including El Jefe himself.

Luca tightened his arm around Harper. Though she had to be in pain as well as freezing, she insisted upon staying until the girl was found. Her concern for the girl touched him, and he felt his heart turn over at her generosity of spirit.

When Stacy and Matt brought the girl out of the bunker next, she ran to Harper and wept.

"One of them is her brother," Harper said, gesturing to the group of men Matt and Stacy had rounded up, "but he didn't protect her." She soothed the slender girl who couldn't have been more than eighteen.

"It'll be okay," Luca assured her. "My team will make sure she gets somewhere safe."

"You can count on it," Stacy said gently. "I know of a place that takes care of girls with no place to go."

Luca's worry over Harper had stretched his patience beyond the breaking point, turning his voice brusque when all he wanted to do was to confess his love to her. Glancing around the group, he said, "We need to get you home. Now."

"I won't argue with you," Stacy returned.

Nash had retrieved one of the snowmobiles, and though

Luca would have preferred a truck, he bundled Harper up as warmly as he could and settled her on the back of the vehicle. "It's going to be cold," he warned.

She smiled wanly. "Don't worry about me."

But he did.

Her lips were blue, and her shivering had intensified. Bruises and abrasions covered nearly every inch of her face. Dried blood crusted around her nostrils and the sides of her mouth. She'd taken a beating but didn't complain of the pain. That wasn't who she was.

"You need to go to the hospital."

She shook her head. "I need to go home. To Danny."

The resolve in her eyes told him that arguing would do no good, so he remained quiet and concentrated on getting her back to the ranch house as quickly as possible.

The trip took longer than he'd wished. With Harper pressed tightly against him, he felt her every breath, every tremble as an icy wind buffeted them. He knew she was in a bad way when she didn't protest as he carried her to the house and up the stairs to her room.

"Hot shower first."

"I need to see Danny," she said the moment he put her on her feet.

"Pardon me for saying so, but you'll scare him out of a full year's growth the way you look right now. Let Ginny help you get cleaned up."

With a startled look, she walked to the mirror above her dresser and gasped. "Okay, a shower it is."

While Ginny helped Harper, Luca looked in on Danny and then checked in with Tommy.

"Everything's okay here," Tommy announced.

Luca clasped the young man's shoulder and gave a brief rundown of the night's action. Tommy gave a low whistle.

"Is Dawson still locked up?" Luca asked.

Tommy nodded. "You better believe it. Sir," he tacked on as he shuffled his feet. "Miss Harper? She all right?"

"She will be."

Luca hoped he was right. Harper had not only been beat up, she'd also suffered from bitter cold. He wanted to wrap her and Danny in his arms and protect them from all harm, but he recognized the impossibility of that.

What the future held, he didn't know. Dare he hope that he and Harper and Danny could make a family?

Harper stood under a hot shower for a full fifteen minutes. When she emerged, she gave herself a critical look in the mirror. She still looked pretty rough around the edges, but at least her hair was no longer matted to her head with blood and her cheeks had a little color to them.

She gave a sigh of pleasure when she pulled on clean clothes. The clothes she'd been wearing were a total loss, and she put them in a pile to be discarded.

Without Luca, she had no doubt that she'd be dead. Though he would deny it, he was a real-life hero. Even when he was much younger, he'd risked incurring the Judge's wrath to save her from a beating.

How had she ever thought she'd stopped loving him?

Ginny checked her over. "You've got some pretty deep bruises, but I don't feel anything broken. Except your nose. It's going to look like you went a round with a boxing champ. You ought to be in the hospital."

Harper frowned. "You sound like Luca."

"Let me put some salve on those bruises and cuts." After treating Harper's abrasions and scrapes, Ginny pronounced that she'd probably live.

Harper gave her new friend a quick hug. "Thank you.

You've been great." Then she went to find Luca and Danny waiting for her downstairs. "Better?" she mouthed to Luca, spreading out her arms. She wanted another opinion before she surprised her son.

He nodded and his lips formed the word "Some."

She supposed the half-hearted answer would have to do.

As if sensing her presence, Danny turned toward her. "Mommy, you're hurt," he said, his eyes filling with tears as he took in the bruises on her face.

"I'm okay now that I'm here with you." She knelt and hugged him to her.

Her little boy clung to her tightly. "You're not going anywhere again, are you?" he asked.

"Not without you."

Danny's arms trembled with the effort of squeezing her.

Tears stung her eyes as she thought of how terrified he must have been. "I'm okay, sweetheart," she whispered. "I promise."

After a hot meal and a short nap, Harper felt like a new woman. She was still sore and wouldn't be surprised if she had a few broken ribs, but they would heal on their own.

When she went downstairs, she heard a commotion in the ranch yard. Luca's team had returned with the cartel members, all of whom looked the worse for wear. Though she'd met Luca's friends only briefly, she'd been impressed with their resolve. It didn't take much deduction to guess that they had treated the bad guys none too gently. Luca and his team were about to transport them to the sheriff's office, along with Chuck Dawson.

Once again, Luca tried to persuade her to go to the hospital.

She shook her head. "I'm staying here," she said. "Danny

needs me. He's been through enough with all that's happened. I won't leave him alone. Not again."

The steadfastness in her voice reminded him of how she had fought alongside him. Over the course of the last week, she'd displayed an unflinching courage that had manifested itself over and over.

"I'll be back as soon as I can. In the meantime, Ginny's here. She'll look after you."

With another shake of her head, she said, "Ginny's got a son who needs her. She needs to get back to him. The bad guys are on their way to jail. There's no one left who wants to hurt Danny and me."

She was right, but Luca couldn't help his frown. He didn't like leaving her and Danny alone, but as she'd said, the bad guys were on their way to jail.

"I'll be back soon," he repeated.

The cells in the sheriff's office were filled to capacity with once tough-looking men who no longer looked so tough. Luca couldn't wait to hand the whole lot of them over to the Feds and let them deal with them.

With Stacy's contacts, four federal officers showed up shortly. The lead agent held out a hand to Luca. "We've been looking for this bunch for a couple of years, and you find them in a matter of days." With disgust, he looked over the motley crew of men, many now sporting black eyes and bruises. "How'd you do it?"

"They took my son," Luca said by way of explanation.

The agent nodded. "Remind me not to get on your bad side."

Luca looked around the sheriff's office. "Where's Davis?" The sheriff had disappeared before the DEA agents had shown up.

"I haven't seen him for a bit," the pretty deputy said. "He probably got called away on something else."

Luca frowned. Davis wasn't the kind to miss an opportunity for glory hogging. If he wasn't there when the federal agents showed up, there had to be a good reason.

Luca didn't like the feeling he was getting. He said his goodbyes to the agents and explained he had to get back to the ranch.

"Thanks for all your help," the lead agent said. "Your company's going to get some publicity for its part in this."

Publicity was the last thing Luca was interested in, but he knew that S&J would benefit from the media coverage. "Thanks."

"This wasn't strictly an S&J operation, but it's still going to bring in some good press," Matt said. "Gideon's going to be doing a happy dance."

Luca clapped his friend on the back. "I can't thank you and the others enough. If it hadn't been for you…"

"None of that," Stacy said. "Taking out scum like that was pure pleasure."

"You got that right," Brett added as he and the others began loading their gear in the truck. "Sure want to thank you for a rip-roaring time."

"Yeah," Nash added. "Haven't had this much fun since we were in the Sandbox."

"You each put it on the line for me and my family," Luca said. "There aren't words—"

Matt gave his friend a one-armed hug. "Then don't try. You're a brother." More hugs were shared, and the four comrades took off.

Luca climbed into his truck and started back to the ranch. He couldn't say why, but urgency had him pressing down harder than usual on the accelerator. No reason to feel uneasy, he assured himself. Harper and Danny were tucked in the house while the bad guys were tucked in cells. Still, it bothered him that the sheriff wasn't there.

Something nagged at him, a dangling thread waiting to be tied off, an insistent voice that kept whispering in his ear, telling him that this wasn't over, telling him that he was missing something, something important.

But what?

The cartel members had been rounded up. They wouldn't be seeing the outside of prison for a long time. Maybe never. Still, his mind fired off shots that refused to quiet. One question in particular ricocheted in his brain. How had the cartel operated in the area for so long without arousing any suspicion?

Yes, Chuck had been helping, but he lacked the brain power and organizational skills to run the operation. Had there been someone else spearheading the entire thing, someone who could operate under the radar without drawing suspicion to himself?

Luca pulled his thoughts to a halt. That made sense. It made a lot of sense. But who would have the know-how and the connections to pull it off? Someone with a lot of clout. As far as he knew, there was no one who wielded that much power in the area. The Judge had been the most influential man in the community for more than two decades. But he had a reputation for law and order, especially when it came to drug-related crimes. Anyone brought before him on a drug charge did his best to get a new judge or just accepted his fate of a lengthy prison sentence.

For each question, two more sprang up. He tried to clear his mind, to see the picture as a whole. Fact: the cartel had been operating in the area. Fact: Chuck Dawson had been part of it. Fact: everyone else involved was now locked up.

There was no longer any reason to be concerned for Harper and Danny. So why were tendrils of doubt crawling up his spine to settle at the base of his neck? Why hadn't they disappeared with the clank of the jail cell signaling that the bad guys had been locked away? Over the years, Luca had learned to trust his gut. It hadn't let him down. Not when he was deployed in Afghanistan. Not in his work for S&J.

Piece by piece, he went through the events of the last few days. Each one fit neatly in place. Except for one. The sheriff's visit at the hospital. What was it he'd said? Something about not having much to go on since Danny couldn't give a description of the kidnappers because they were wearing masks.

A beat and then another passed. Neither Luca nor Harper had said anything about masks in their statements to the sheriff. So how had he known about them?

To Harper's surprise, she opened the back door to the sheriff at the insistent knock.

Caar Davis grabbed her hands and held them. "Thank goodness you're all right."

She nodded, withdrawing her hands. "Thanks to Luca and his friends, everyone's all right."

His expression soured for a moment, and she wondered if he'd taken her words as a slight.

Uninvited, he stepped past her into the kitchen. Though she was tired to the point of exhaustion, she offered coffee and was relieved when he turned it down.

"This is a great house," he said, looking around the kitchen. "With a little fixing up, it could be a real showplace."

"I like it as it is." His observation confused her. What business was it of his what the house looked like?

"I could see myself living here." He pulled out a chair, sat and squared one leg over the other, making himself at home.

"Oh?"

"Yeah. You and I have something good going."

She made a point of remaining standing, hoping he'd take the hint that she wasn't in the mood for chit-chat. "Caar… I'm sorry if I've given you the wrong idea, but I think of you as a friend. Nothing more."

"I was afraid you'd say that. Things could have been good between us. Real good."

Something in his tone bothered her. "If you don't mind, I'm tired. Danny and I both need to rest." When he made no move to get up, she added, "I think it's time for you to leave."

He held up his hands in a conceding gesture. "Sorry for all that." His conciliatory tone caused her to relax. "If it's okay, I'd like to take you up on the offer of coffee if it still stands."

"Of course." She set about making the coffee. "Instant okay?"

"Sure."

When she handed him the cup of steaming liquid, he smiled. "Thanks."

"No problem."

"Aren't you going to have some?"

"Not now. I need to see to my son." A few minutes passed, and when she noted his empty cup, she tried to urge him to leave. "If you're done…"

He stood. "I'm glad you and the boy are all right."

"Thank you." Had he ever referred to Danny by name? Or had he always referred to him as "the boy"?

"It's too bad he couldn't give us a real description of the men who took him."

She bristled. "He did the best he could considering they were wearing masks." She paused, thinking back. The conversation caused a frisson of memory to ripple through her. When Caar had visited her in the hospital, he'd said something about masks, yet neither she nor Luca had mentioned them.

Was Caar involved? No. She was wrong. She had to be. Up until now, she had been only annoyed that he wouldn't leave. Now that annoyance was turning to alarm and the alarm to fear. "I don't know what's gotten into you, Caar, but you need to leave. Now." An uneasy feeling shivered through her at the predatory way he eyed her.

Danny, who had been in the den with a book, ran into the room. Obviously sensing something in the air, he looked from Harper to the sheriff and back again. "Mommy, are you all right?"

"I'm fine. Go back and finish reading your book."

Caar clamped a hand on her son's shoulder. "He's fine right here." A rueful expression settled on his face. "I was wondering if you remembered the masks. Stupid mistake on my part."

She decided to bluff it out. "I don't know what you're talking about."

He gave her a shrewd look that darkened his eyes. "Oh, I think you do."

She took a step back. Another.

"I made a mistake in mentioning masks that day at the hospital."

She started to deny it but realized it was too late. "How

did you know they were wearing masks?" She didn't give him time to form a reply and answered her own question in the next breath. "You were part of it."

Comprehension turned to horror. Harper felt the same kind of disgust she had upon learning of Chuck's part in the plot. How had both men managed to deceive her so thoroughly? Though she'd never felt anything beyond a mild friendship between her and Caar, she had never suspected he'd be involved in the nasty business of drug running. "Why?"

"Why do you think?"

"Money."

"Ah! You're on a roll," he said.

Her skin tingling with fear, she wished she had kept Luca's gun. She looked at her son, who'd thrown off the sheriff's clutches and backed against the sink. She had to get him away. "Luca will be back soon," she said.

"Oh, yes. The great and mighty Luca. It's too bad he had to come back."

"What are you talking about? Luca's never done anything to you."

"You and the boy and I could have made a real fine family." He shook his head. "With you and me married, it would have fallen to me to run the ranch. I could have made this place my headquarters for the drug running."

"And I was just supposed to go along with you and play the little woman?"

"Why not? I'm a catch." A prideful grin split his lips.

She let her revulsion show. All the while they'd been talking, she had been inching her way forward, putting herself between the sheriff and Danny.

Caar pulled his weapon. "Might as well save yourself the trouble. The boy's gonna die right alongside you."

"You won't get away with it."

"Who's going to suspect me? For all anyone knows, I was wounded trying to protect you and the boy. And when it comes out that your old man was in with the cartel, nobody's gonna grieve for you much."

"You're lying."

"Am I? Think about it. The cartel was operating right under his nose. You can't be so naïve that you didn't suspect something. How do you think the dealers knew about the bunker? Someone had to tell them. Someone like the illustrious judge."

She had never defended her father for anything, but she didn't believe Caar's accusation. "He never let anyone get away with anything. People referred to him as Mr. Law and Order."

"Your old man was losing money hand-over-fist with the ranch and had been for years. Everything was going up in price. How did you think he kept it going?"

"He took out a loan from the bank." But she heard the doubt in her voice.

"Banks aren't in the habit of giving out money to failing enterprises. And that's what the ranch was. And all of a sudden, there's a big influx of cash. Past loans were paid off. New equipment suddenly shows up. Where do you think that cash came from?"

"I didn't…" Hadn't she wondered sometimes how the Judge had afforded the new barn and tractor and other things he'd recently purchased for the ranch? But never had she considered that he was part of the drug trade.

"The Judge threw the book at anyone caught dealing in drugs," she said at last.

"That's right. Except for members of the cartel. Somehow, they skated with only a slap on the wrist."

"What do you want, Caar?"

"If you'd fallen into line, we'd be married by now, and I'd be running the ranch. As it is, we'll have to do things the hard way."

What did he mean?

"You can walk away from this," she said. "It's not too late."

"Don't give me that. You and I both know it's way too late. I have to get out of here, but I'm not going without making sure you pay for what you did."

"What *I* did? What are you talking about?"

"You had to go get your precious ranger and bring him back here. I could tell the way the wind was blowing when I saw you with him in the hospital."

She glanced toward her son. Her brave boy whom she loved more than life itself. "You don't have to hurt Danny."

"You never could see past that kid." Davis's lips curled with disgust.

"No. I couldn't." She put her son behind her. "You're a toad, Caar. You always have been. From the time we were in grade school together. I thought you'd changed. The only thing that's changed about you is that you're a bigger toad than you were."

His face reddened. At the same time, a prominent vein in his forehead pulsed violently. "You always did think you were too good for me." He struck her in the face.

"Turns out I was right."

He made to backhand her again, but she sidestepped. Taken by surprise, he didn't have time to block her move when she brought her knee up and rammed it into his groin.

Making a strangled noise, he staggered.

She and Danny had to get out of there, but she hadn't counted on Caar having enough remaining strength to grab her wrist and yank her to him. He was a powerful man and was crushing the delicate bones in her wrist.

"Danny! Run!"

Instead of doing as she instructed, her son kicked Caar in the shin then bit his hand.

Harper wanted to applaud him for his bravery even as she wished he'd obeyed her. Fear for her son lent her sufficient strength to wrench her arm from the sheriff's grasp, but this time he turned his force against Danny, hauling him up by his shirt collar and pulling him against him.

"Little brat. You always were in the way."

Danny squirmed in Caar's arms, but he was just a small boy, and Caar was a heavily built man.

Harper tried to claw at the sheriff's face, but he used Danny as a shield.

"Do as I say, or I'll really hurt him," Caar said. Hatred oozed from every syllable. How had she not seen how odious he was?

"Now get over here." He pulled a knife from its scabbard and held it to Danny's neck. As the first pinprick of blood showed, rage roiled within her. She wanted to attack him with everything she had, but that was likely to get her son's throat sliced.

Be smart.

"Mommy!" Danny cried. "I'm scared!"

"It'll be all right," she said. She'd tried never to lie to Danny and prayed that she wasn't lying now. Somehow, someway, they would find a way out of this.

If she did as Caar ordered, she feared she'd give up her only leverage, but there was no way she'd let the sheriff use his knife on Danny again. With an air of feigned defeat, she closed the short distance between her and the man who held her son. "You have me. Now let Danny go."

"You're stupider than I thought if you think I'll let either of you go. You're my insurance out of this place."

Harper bared her teeth. "If you hurt him, Luca will come after you like fury. There's no place you can run, no place you can hide that he won't find you."

"When he sees that I've got you and the kid, your big tough ranger won't be so big or so tough."

With a burst of strength, she yanked Danny away, grabbed his hand and ran. She knew they couldn't outrun Caar, not with his longer stride. She opened the first door she came to—the downstairs powder room—and pulled her son inside. Fortunately, the door had an old-fashioned metal lock that couldn't easily be broken. She turned it and tried to think.

"Mommy?" The single word was a question, but she heard the fear behind it.

"We just have to hold on until Luca gets here." She took Danny's hand in hers and squeezed, trying to reassure him…and herself. His hand trembled inside her own, but he squared his small shoulders. "We can do it," he said. "Luca will come."

Never had she been prouder of her son.

Please, Lord, let it be in time. The prayer steadied her even as Caar was hacking at the door with his knife.

She looked around the tiny bathroom. What weapons did she have? A bar of soap. A couple of towels. Her gaze paused on a plastic container of ammonia and a spray bottle of cleanser with bleach.

Whether born of inspiration or desperation, an idea came to her. She poured the ammonia into the bottle of bleach. Holding her breath against the toxic fumes, she grabbed a couple of towels and handed one to Danny. "Wrap this around your face as tight as you can."

"What're you going to do?"

"Buy us some time." She hoped.

Cracks showed in the door. It would be only a minute, two at the most, before Caar broke it down.

She held the spray bottle in front of her, then adjusted the towel until it covered as much of her face as possible. She couldn't cover her eyes, not if she were to aim her improvised weapon.

Even with her face mostly covered, the fumes seeped into her eyes and mouth and nose.

Hold on.

The door splintered. A booted foot was the first thing she saw. She steadied herself and aimed the makeshift weapon at the sheriff as he crashed his way through the door.

He opened his mouth. Whatever he'd been going to say was lost as the spray hit his face. He spat. Coughed. Put a hand to his eyes, inadvertently rubbing the toxic mixture in even more.

"You…" While sputtering out a series of words, he thrashed around, in the process dropping his gun.

Harper snatched it up and held it on him.

"What're you going to do with that?" Though tears were streaming down his face, he continued to advance on her and Danny.

And despite everything that had happened in the last week, despite the danger to Danny and herself, could she shoot him?

FIFTEEN

Luca pulled up in the ranch yard and took off for the back entrance of the house. When a scream tore through the kitchen and the hallway, he doubled his speed.

In the small bathroom stood Harper, a gun steady in her hand, Danny behind her. An acrid odor stung his nostrils, and he put a kerchief over his mouth and nose.

Davis lay on the floor, agony written in every line of his face.

"She nearly blinded me," the sheriff said, his voice a combination of disbelief and a whine.

His reddened eyes and splotchy skin were mute evidence of a chemical burn.

"Mommy took care of him," Danny said. The excitement Luca might have expected from his son was absent, though. Freckles stood out on his nearly white face, and he kept a tight hold on Harper's free hand.

"I can see that." Luca's gaze searched Harper's. "Looks like Danny's right and that you took care of him."

"I did my best."

Gently, he took her chin in his hands. "Did he do that?" he asked, gesturing to her cheek, which now sported fresh abrasions.

"Yeah. Caar got in a slap or two. It's not too bad," she said and then negated the words by wincing sharply.

Luca fixed a hard gaze on the sheriff.

Life was made up of shades of gray. Light grays and dark grays, with a few blacks and whites thrown in for good measure. Right now, Luca was seriously considering dipping into one of the darker grays and carrying through with his threat.

Harper must have read his thoughts for she shifted her gaze to Danny, silently pleading with Luca not to do anything in front of their son. She was right. Though seriously tempted, he backed off.

"I need a doctor," Davis moaned, causing Luca to grin. He'd be real popular with the lowlifes in a federal pen, especially when they learned he'd been a cop.

Chemical burns could be incredibly painful, but Luca couldn't find it in himself to feel sorry for the man. Davis had planned on killing Harper and Danny. No, there'd be no sympathy. Not from him.

"I'm taking you to the hospital," he told Harper.

"I don't need—"

"This makes twice that you've been beaten up in the last two days. It's time to admit that you're not invincible."

She pointed to Davis. "What about him?"

"We'll take him with us."

Indifferent to the sheriff's injury, Luca tied him up and dumped him into the pickup bed. He then helped Harper and Danny into warm jackets and tucked them into the truck cab. After securing their seat belts around them, he rounded the truck, started it up and pointed it toward town.

Luca took her to the emergency room entrance, where she was whisked away to a cubicle. As for the sheriff, Luca gave a terse explanation and then called the sheriff's office.

The irony of calling the SO to send someone to arrest the actual sheriff wasn't lost on him.

Harper refused treatment until Danny was examined first.

"He has one tiny nick," the doctor said. "A superhero bandage should take care of it just right." Danny was so enthralled with the Superman bandage that he scarcely noticed the prick of the needle administering antibiotics.

Only after she knew her son was all right and a nurse took him to Luca did she consent to be examined.

"Seems like you're getting to be a regular visitor around here," the doctor reproved as he looked at Harper, checking for internal as well as external injuries. "Someone was looking out for you. No concussion and no broken ribs. Just don't get into any more fights." He prescribed pain medication and told her she could get dressed.

Ten minutes later, Luca joined them. "Your fighting days are over."

She glared at him. He made it sound like she went around looking for fights.

"My mommy's the best," Danny said. "She took care of us when the sheriff tried to hurt us."

The doctor raised a brow. "That's a story I need to hear."

"I'm sure it will be making the rounds," Harper said wryly. The community was a small one. She didn't doubt that everyone in town would know about Davis's involvement in the drug trade by the end of the day. And the Judge's.

Pain lanced through her at what the Judge had done. She tried to brush it off with a shrug—people would think what they would—but she couldn't help grieving that he had stooped to working with drug runners.

"Let's get you home," Luca said.

After she was wheeled out of the hospital, Luca lifted her with infinite gentleness and put her in the cab of his truck.

"Luca, you should have seen it," Danny said once they were on their way back to the ranch. "Mommy was totally awesome."

Luca gave her a sideways look. "I've always thought so."

She blushed. That hadn't changed.

"I think she could be an MMA fighter."

Both Harper and Luca laughed.

"What do you know about MMA fighting, young man?" she asked.

"I heard about it on television."

After a few minutes, when Danny dozed off to sleep, she asked, "What do you think will happen to Davis?"

"I'm guessing he's going to be real popular in the federal pen."

By the time they reached the ranch, she was well and truly hurting. "Wait here," Luca said as he picked up Danny. When he returned from carrying their son to the house, Luca lifted her from the truck.

"I can walk on my own," she said.

"I'm sure you can, but you don't have to. Not while I'm here." He ignored her protests and carried her into the house and up the stairs. "It's bed for you. I'll clean up."

She didn't argue.

After she emerged from the shower, Harper listened to nonstop chatter from Danny, who had awakened from his nap. "You were right, Mommy. Luca saved us."

Wrapped in a thick robe, she sat in bed, propped against the headboard with her son nestled at her side.

"Just like you did," he added. She drew him closer to her and gave thanks for the precious gift of her son.

Luca appeared a few minutes later, bearing a tray laden with bowls of chili, crackers and wedges of cheese. The three of them ate in Harper's room.

Surreptitiously, she studied the strong lines of Luca's profile. The danger was over, as well as his reason for being here. What did that mean for him? What did it mean for her and Danny? She no longer feared that he would try to take Danny away from her. They would share custody. Danny needed a father in his life, just as the father needed the son.

When Luca returned after taking Danny to bed, she smiled at him. "You're getting pretty good at the dad thing." Her expression sobered. "You saved our lives today."

"I'd say that you saved yourself."

"Without you…" Her voice thickened, and she cleared her throat. "Without you, Danny and I could both be dead." Her smile of a few moments ago died abruptly. "The Judge was in on it, too." Her voice shook over the last words. "How could I not have known?"

"Give yourself a break. No one, not even me, thought the Judge could be involved in drug smuggling."

"It was right there in front of me, and I couldn't see it." It seemed that her life as she'd known it had been a sham. First Chuck and now the Judge had deceived her and betrayed her. Why hadn't she seen what was right in front of her? Had she deliberately ignored the signs?

"The Judge was a smart man. Smart and clever. He didn't let anyone see what he didn't want them to."

"I was his daughter. I should have known. I knew the ranch was in trouble, but, somehow, he kept it going." Her laugh was hollow. "I should say that drugs kept it going. He was selling the very thing he abhorred."

"He was desperate."

She pulled back enough to stare at Luca. "Are you defending him?"

"No. I'm just saying desperate men sometimes do desperate things."

She couldn't stay at the ranch any longer, not when she knew where the money to keep it going had come from. There were plenty of ranchers who'd be willing to buy the land and to take the cattle and horses off her hands.

Whatever profit she made would go to help those who were addicted to the drugs that the Judge's perfidy had helped put on the streets.

When she told Luca of her plans, he nodded approvingly. "That's a great idea. Where will you live?"

"I'm going to keep the house where Chuck and Vera lived and a few acres. That's plenty big enough for Danny and me."

He stroked her cheek with the back of his hand, the lightly callused flesh creating a sweet friction against her softer skin.

It was the warmest, most loving gesture she'd ever known. She curved her arms around his neck and nestled into him and pushed aside the inevitable.

The time would come to say goodbye. Luca had a life to get back to.

For now, she would cherish this time together and hold it tight. There would be time—plenty of time—for loneliness to sink in when he left. She wouldn't think of that.

She put a finger to his lips. Words could be spoken later. There would be tears, she was certain. Hers. But she refused to let them have their way now.

She pressed a kiss over his lips and let it linger. If wishes came true, she would find the words that would convince him to stay. If only.

The custody issues would be worked out. It wasn't as though they lived so far apart that they couldn't share time with Danny.

She'd hoped for something different, but that wasn't to be. Was Luca filled with the same would've, could'ves and should'ves as she was?

If she would've stood up to her father six years ago.

If she could've reached Luca and told him about Danny.

And the should've? She should've never let him leave all those years ago. "I guess this is goodbye." Disappointment washed through her and pulled tight when he didn't object.

She heard a small voice coming from the doorway. "Mommy, I don't want Luca to go away. He's my best friend." Danny ran into the room.

She and Luca turned to each other, sharing a look that both asked and answered an unspoken question. It was time to tell Danny who Luca really was. "We have something to tell you," she said to her son. Why was the truth so difficult to say?

"I'm glad Luca's your best friend. But he's something else, too." She swallowed past the lump that lodged in her throat. "Luca is your father."

"You mean he's my daddy?"

"That's exactly what I mean."

Danny ran to Luca and threw his arms around his waist. "If you're my daddy, then I'm your little boy."

Luca swung Danny into his arms. "That's right. How do you feel about it?"

"I feel great." Danny smacked a wet, noisy kiss on Luca's check. "That means we can be family."

Love filled her heart for father and son. But nothing had been settled, and she steeled herself for what she had to say to Luca. "I'll bring Danny to you next weekend."

She prayed he would say that this didn't have to be good-bye, that they would find a way to be together. For always.

But the only word he uttered was "Fine."

Only it wasn't fine. It wasn't fine at all.

In the small shotgun-style house that was home, Luca slammed a fist into his palm. He wasn't very good company these days. His friends had started giving him a wide berth at work, and he didn't blame them.

A week had passed since he'd last seen Harper and Danny, a week of loneliness and self-pity. It had been the longest week of his life.

What was really keeping them apart? An old misunderstanding? They'd laid that to rest. Custody issues could be resolved.

No, it was neither of those. It was something far more basic. He was afraid. Afraid that if he told Harper of his feelings for her, she would reject them. Reject him.

And he didn't know if he could bear that.

He'd been a ranger. Rangers led the way, he reminded himself. Maybe it was time he started doing just that.

When he took off early for home to be there when they arrived, no one complained. There were still custody details to work out. How did you share a child? It wasn't as though Danny was a piece of pie that you split down the middle. He deserved a home, a real one.

When mother and son arrived, Danny ran and threw himself at Luca. Luca swept him up in his arms. Little boy arms circled his neck and squeezed, just as little boy smells wrapped their way around his heart. He could have held this child forever, but Danny grew restless and wiggled free.

Luca shifted his gaze to Harper. "You look good," he

said. Most of the bruising had faded, and she'd regained some of the weight she'd lost.

He felt her gaze on him, could almost hear the questions in her eyes, questions neither of them had the courage to answer.

And, in that instant, he knew that this was what mattered. Harper and Danny mattered. What was more, he mattered to them. The rest of it was only logistics. They'd make it work. If he had to leave S&J, he would do so. He didn't think it would come to that, as the company was more than lenient about family matters.

His throat tightened with emotion. He squeezed his eyes shut to block out the loneliness of the last six years and the loneliness of the next. Wrapping his arms around Harper and Danny, he inhaled deeply, wanting to imprint this moment forever into his memory.

Danny wrapped his arms around Luca's legs. When both Harper and Luca remained silent, their son said, "I want to live with both of you. At the same time. There's plenty of room at the ranch," he told Luca, the hopeful note in his voice tearing Luca's heart.

When both Harper and Luca remained silent, their son said, "Can we?"

"I wish we could," Luca told Danny, but his gaze remained on Harper.

"It's more complicated than that," she said at last.

"Why?" Danny and Luca asked in unison.

Why?

The word startled Harper. Why *was* it more complicated?

"It...just is," she said and winced at the inadequacy of

her reply. "Your father and I were together once. But we aren't any longer."

"Why?" This from Luca.

She shot him a dirty look. "You know why. For one thing, we aren't married any longer."

"Why?" he asked. "Why aren't we married?"

She flashed him a look. "You're just making this harder," she said in a terse whisper.

"No. I'm trying to make it right. I love you. I love Danny. And I think you love me. I don't see any reason we can't be together."

Her heart soared at his words...yet it was all happening too fast. It had been barely two weeks since he'd come back into her life. A gamut of confusing emotions raced through her. "I need time to sort things out." Time to sort herself out.

"What do you need to sort out?" Luca asked.

"Yeah, Mommy. What do you need to sort out?" Danny echoed, sounding so much like his father that she wanted to cry. At the same time, she wanted to wrap her arms around them and never let go.

"You have a job for one thing," she told Luca. "You can't just quit doing what you love."

"I can do my job from there. And if I can't, I'll find something else to do." He sent a teasing smile her way. "What else do you have to sort out?"

"It takes time to plan a wedding."

"Tell me something. Do you want something big and fancy?"

She shuddered at the idea. "No."

"That's what I thought." He gave a satisfied smile. "We can do it at the ranch. I know a justice of the peace who will come to us. Danny can be my best man. I'll invite a few friends, and you can do the same. Marry me, Harper. Again."

The two men in her life looked at her with such pleading… and she couldn't say no. Not when her heart clamored for her to say *yes*. A slow smile spread across her lips as happiness coursed through her. Flames of hope, which had flickered and guttered only moments ago, suddenly erupted into a bonfire.

She divided a helpless look between them. "Yes. A thousand times yes."

"Is it for real?" Danny asked. "I'm going to have a mommy and a daddy, and we're all going to live together?"

"It's for real," she said, her heart stretching to the breaking point to hold the fullness of family and love. "It's very much for real."

She turned slightly and brushed a kiss over Luca's mouth, at the same time resting her hand on Danny's shoulder.

Luca covered her hand with his own. "I have loved you from the beginning."

"And I will love you until the end." With that, she kissed him again. A long, slow kiss that said more than words ever could.

* * * * *

If you loved this action-packed story,
then check out other gripping suspense stories
by Jane M. Choate.

Available now from Love Inspired Suspense!

And discover more at LoveInspired.com.

Dear Reader,

Thank you for joining me on another love journey. Luca and Harper's love path did not run smoothly. Kidnapping, betrayal, loss of faith and other perils faced them, but they remained strong, remained true to their values.

Holding on to our beliefs requires commitment, courage and, most of all, faith. Knowing that the Lord is on our side can and will see us through the most challenging trials, the most heartbreaking persecutions. Though others may abandon us, though others may leave us forsaken, the Lord will not. He is on our side.

With gratitude to each of you for sharing Harper and Luca's story with me and with faith in the Lord,

Jane

Harlequin® Reader Service

Enjoyed your book?

Try the perfect subscription for Romance readers and get more great books like this delivered right to your door.

See why over 10+ million readers have tried Harlequin Reader Service.

Start with a Free Welcome Collection with free books and a gift—valued over $20.

Choose any series in print or ebook. See website for details and order today:

TryReaderService.com/subscriptions